# Fourteen From Four

"Despite the strict confines of the short story, Julia Stoneham creates vivid, memorable characters whose lives move, intrigue and absorb you. Her compassion for humankind together with her eye for the telling details capture your sympathy for her unusual and appealing cast. You won't forget Muriel, Orla, Sybilla, Connie and the rest."

*Kay Dunbar, Ways With Words*

"Subtle and surprising...a writer with insight."

*Penelope Wilton*

"This whets the appetite for Julia Stoneham's fiction."

*Pat Jackson, film director*

Julia Stoneham

# Fourteen From Four

*a collection of short stories*
*first broadcast on radio four*

British Library Cataloguing in Publication Data
A catalogue record for this book is available from the British Library

ISBN  0-9550436-0-3

Typeset by Amolibros, Milverton, Somerset
This book production has been managed by Amolibros
Printed and bound by T J International Ltd, Padstow, Cornwall

# Contents

# Introduction

It sounds so simple – a short story – a story that is short. From the "stream of consciousness", through the memoir or the fragment of biography to the probing delicacy of Katherine Mansfield, the wit of James Thurber or the crackling provocation of Ian McEwan's first published fiction – short stories, all of them. Is there any other area in literature that boasts such diversity?

The radio short story, however, requires a specific treatment. It will almost certainly be broadcast on Radio Four, must appeal to that audience – and not offend it. Ten years ago, when "Frangipani Experience" was originally offered, it was rejected on the grounds that some listeners might find it too risqué! This constraint also applies to certain expletives which, if not deleted by the writer will be, by the producer. One learns to find alternatives.

The recorded story must have an exact running time in order to fit the slot available to it. The announcements, fore and aft, absorb some of this time, leaving the writer with precisely fourteen minutes. Radio Three sometimes uses short fiction as a filler during intervals in the transmission of live concerts and these readings may be slightly longer. My first short story was commissioned for Radio Three by Piers Plowright and read by the late Joan Hart. "Mirror, Mirror" ran for twenty minutes – luxury.

Inevitably some ideas prove to be either too complex or too slight to fit the radio story time-scale and have to be discarded.

Having found a story that is suitable for the number of words available for the telling of it, it can still prove difficult to hit the target of fourteen minutes. There is always the possibility that the actor recording the story will take it either faster or more slowly than anticipated. This happened to me when Philip Franks read "Solitaire". In "real life" Philip speaks very quickly. Expecting a fast delivery, I indulged myself when I heard he was to be our reader and added a few sentences to the text. At the recording session Philip surprised us by taking the reading quite slowly so that we ended up being slightly "over". On other occasions, when an actor has read faster than expected, we have been marginally "under" – but only narrowly, and any minor nipping and tucking is expertly dealt with by the technicians. However, if a short story is properly written, nothing should be there that is not important to it and this makes cutting difficult. Extensive cutting will very quickly unbalance the construction. So careful timing, during the writing, is essential.

All of these factors add to the challenges of producing short stories for radio and to the pleasure of writing them.

# Leo's War

"Leo's War" was recorded at the Guildhall in Bath as part of the 2005 festival. It was broadcast the following week on BBC Radio Four. The producer was Sara Davies and the reader was Bill Wallis.

I had almost called our mother back. I had almost told her. Then the bedroom doorway was empty and I heard her going down the creaking stairs.

The dare, the challenge, was to make the dangerous journey from Aune Beach to Michaelmas via the undercliff. It must be done fast, leaving Aune at low-water slack and, as the first waves of the in-coming tide regained the cliffs, reaching the mole that provided a haven for the half-dozen crab boats working out of Michaelmas. It was forbidden. So it tempted us, enticed us, scared us.

We had become aware of it soon after we arrived at Aune where, because of the war, we were living in a rented cottage with our mother while our father, in our shuttered London house, endured the blitz. We were weekly boarders at a private school, arriving home on Friday evenings and departing after tea on Sundays. Because of this we were considered by the village children to be outsiders and were regarded with something closer to suspicion than friendship.

The challenge, a rite of passage, had to be met by succeeding generations of local boys before they reached their teens and although I, the youngest in our family, was only nine years old, my brothers were twelve and fourteen, making us almost the only boys in our age group not to have accepted it. As a consequence we were increasingly taunted with what, to the locals, was beginning to look like cowardice. It was important to us that our family honour was respected, and although our father had forbidden us to add to our mother's anxieties by misbehaving, the challenge must be met and soon, though failure could result in disaster and I was barely robust or mature enough to undertake it.

Tom, the oldest of us, was sandy-haired and sturdy. He played rugby with a dangerous vigour. George was brainy. Although short, he was wiry and nimble. He had the same golden eyes and sleek, dark hair as our mother. I was a mixture of my brothers but lacked the advantages of either. Blond, without Tom's stamina, slight, without George's agility, I was uncertain which of them I most wished to emulate. It was enough, then, just to keep up with them without too often beseeching them to "Wait for me!"

The occasions when the challenge could be undertaken occurred only twice in each year—when a spring tide coincided with the vernal or autumnal equinox. Then, for a few days in March and again in September, the sea rose higher and fell lower than at any other time, inundating the salt marsh at high-water, then sluicing out, exposing acres of unfamiliar mudflats and miles of hard, ribbed sand, while the rocks of the undercliff, which even at low tide were usually covered, became briefly visible. Dragons' backs, protruding into the sea and leaving, for an hour or so, a narrow strip of weed-strewn foreshore extending around the headland that separates Aune from Michaelmas.

Once a group of local boys had mistimed their attempt. A crabber had spotted them, already waist-deep in turbulent water, clinging to the undercliff. The man had rowed in as close as he dared, thrown a rope to the panicking children and hauled them, one by one, out through the surf to his pitching boat. It had been dangerous. One of the boys had lacerated a leg, another was concussed.

Later they had sat bruised, embarrassed and shivering in the cottage hospital, blankets round their shoulders, mugs of hot cocoa between their palms, and been scolded by indignant nurses and tearful parents while their peers scoffed to conceal their relief, and were either secretly grateful that they had already proved themselves or determined to take extra care when their turn came to do so.

It was September when we attempted it. A recent storm had blown itself out leaving a swell still steep enough to drive spray up over the cliffs when the tide was high, and to explode against the reefs at low water.

On Aune beach a group of local boys was engaged in some elaborate, Arthurian game involving spears tipped with silver paper. They climbed and swung among the rusting scaffolding, which—an attempt to deter German invaders—straddled the beach. They watched as my brothers and I crossed the corrugated sand to where the cliffs began. Tom and George consulted their watches, carefully checked the state of the tide and unanimously agreed that we were within a spit of low-water slack. We gathered ourselves.

Our identical oilskin jackets had sou'westers attached by tapes to their collars. They bobbed and flopped against our shoulders as we ran towards the undercliff. Convinced now that the challenge was on, the local boys dropped like monkeys from the scaffolding and scattered, yelling and hooting, towards the path that would take them up, over the headland and down, to the mole where they would assemble, waiting for us to round the point and make our final desperate sprint, possibly through deepening water, to safety. If we failed to appear it would be they who would raise the alarm. All of us knew that because of the formation of the cliffs it was impossible to scale them, and that if we should become cut off by the tide our chances of rescue were small, because no boats were out crabbing in that day's wild sea.

At the base of the cliffs, sculpted by the receding tide, were cold, damp dunes of packed sand. There were pools in which weed and sea anemones shimmered under clear, shallow water. There were starfish and crabs, mussels and periwinkles. Barnacles and limpets stuck fast to rocks overlaid with kelp and sprawling bladderwrack, which slithered and popped underfoot. Troughs of pale, rounded pebbles lay in the gullies between the reefs, shifting under the soles of our rubber boots.

It had looked so easy. Out across the rocks to the point and round it. Then into sight of the mole and the safety of Michaelmas. It was only half a mile! But as we went, crouched, trying not to waste time on stumbling and sliding, urgency nudging towards panic, the challenge seemed to stretch endlessly before us. To our left the dark face of the cliff loomed sheer and dripping, to our right waves boiled among the rocks and surged up the gullies between them, weed spreading like drowned hair. The cliff base was hollowed into cavernous fissures, sea caves twisting upwards, revealing jagged voids that dissolved into darkness.

However much I tried to prevent it the distance between me and my brothers was increasing. Attempting to shorten it I struck closer to the cliff face, and because of this it was I who spotted the parachute. At first I thought it was a drift of wind-blown spume collecting between two ridges of rock. Then I saw the silky folds, the trailing harness and the footprints.

Tom, turning to check on my progress, saw my hesitation and yelled to me, gesticulating at the incoming surf. I must obey him. But as I took a step forward I saw, in the tail of my eye and only feet from me, a figure. I had seen pictures of German pilots and identified at once the leather suit and the flying helmet. The parachutist was, I guessed, a survivor of a distant dogfight my brothers and I had watched that morning, squinting into the low sun and just catching a flash of silver and the plume of spray thrown up as the plane ditched. He stood, where only I could see him, flattened against the cave wall and, to silence me, raised a shaking finger to his lips. His eyes were dark in his wet, white face. "Bitter," he said. "Bitter."

George had seen me stop. He turned and ran back to me, grabbed me by the arm and dragged me on. I struggled and shouted and pointed to the cave. But George was stronger than I and he hauled me away to where Tom was waiting, and the two of them took me by the arms and ran with me, faster and faster, until I could hardly breathe and my feet barely touched the slithery rocks. Once we fell. All three of us sprawling heavily, I struck my head and the sky filled briefly with points of light. Then we were up, Tom urging us on, blood streaming from George's knees. But the mole was in sight! We could see the spear-carriers silhouetted against the sky. Already the tide was lapping the base of the flight of stone steps, each spent wave raising the water level by an inch or so as we splashed through. The village boys grudgingly acknowledged our achievement and, suddenly embarrassed by their toy spears, smirked and slunk away.

Already late for tea we hurried home, knowing how our lateness added to our mother's wartime anxieties, my brothers, as usual, setting a pace that forced me to run in order to keep up with them.

"You mustn't tell mother about the parachute, Leo!"

"But the airman!" I gasped. "He'll drown!" Above my head my brothers exchanged glances. They knew that by now deep water would be surging through the sea caves.

"There was no airman, Leo!"

"There was!"

"No. You banged your head!"

"That was after!"

"Then you imagined him! Anyway, you can't tell mother! Not even about the parachute, 'cos she'd find out where we've been and what we've done! We're not allowed to worry her! We promised Father, Leo. We promised!"

It was true. Our mother's nerves were weak. She shook as she listened to news of the war and at night paced the cottage, fear of the threatened invasion preventing sleep.

As she dressed George's grazed knees and dabbed witch hazel on my forehead our mother scolded Tom for not taking better care of us.

"And look at Leo!" she said, reproachfully. "White as a sheet!" And she reminded Tom of his promise to his father. Tom hung his head but made no excuses.

She bathed me and fed me chicken broth.

In the warmth of my bed I grew drowsy. Our mother, smelling faintly of bath soap, leaned across to switch off the lamp and sat in silence beside me, yellow light from the landing spilling into the dark room. I shut my eyes. He was a German after all… . He had been trying, before he was shot down, to bomb us… . Perhaps I *had* imagined him…

Assuming I had fallen asleep our mother quietly gathered up the soup bowl and the spoon. As she reached the door I said, "What does bitter mean?"

Surprised, she paused to consider. "Well, something that tastes sour. Like a lemon. Or it can mean a person who is sad or disappointed. Or a wind that's very cold." She hesitated. "Unless, of course, you are a German…" She gave a small, thin laugh.

"And then what does it mean?"

"And then it is 'bitte'," she said, lightly, pronouncing the word carefully, recalling a pre-war holiday in the Black Forest. "And it means 'please'." She blew me a kiss from the open doorway.

In my bedroom in London there had been a painting of a small boy saying his prayers. I got out of my bed, knelt and pressed my palms together like the boy in the picture. "Please God, let the airman be safe." I knew he couldn't possibly be. Then I said, "Bitte. Bitte!"

Across the landing our mother moved about in my brothers' bedroom. She must have heard my voice. She said, "Leo?" It would have been so easy to call her back. To tell her. But I held my breath until the stairs creaked as she went down them. A door below was opened and after a moment quietly closed. I lay, while the night wind nosed around the cottage and I knew that I would not tell her. I would not worry her. I felt warm. Strong. And at least as grown up as my brothers.

# Frangipani Experience

"Frangipani Experience" was recorded by BBC Bristol and transmitted in 2002. It was one of five stories with the umbrella title *Small Things*. The reader was Jacqueline Tong and the programme was produced by Christine Hall.

An only child, Sybilla Cartwright had been carefully reared by elderly parents. By the time she reached thirty-five, her acquaintances, had they thought about it, would have considered it unlikely that she would marry. Not that she was unattractive. The care she had always taken of her appearance repaid her now that she was, let's face it, moving towards early middle age.

Sybilla was always in demand as a partner at dinner-dances at her golf or tennis club, where she was considered good company and could be relied upon to look attractive and behave impeccably. The years had turned and though by no means a wallflower, Sybilla had failed to provoke that level of interest among the men she encountered, which had led, in the cases of her fairer sisters, to marriage or even to a serious love affair. She did not compete for male attention, having been raised in the belief that to do so was at best unnecessary and at worst mildly distasteful. Her competitiveness was absorbed by the several sporting activities, tennis, squash, badminton, and especially by golf, at which she excelled.

She was, as far as it is possible for a person to be, unremarkable. The most unusual thing about Sybilla in this permissive day and age was what she privately defined as her "inexperience". It was not a state that she had deliberately sought. It was simply something that had happened. Or, more precisely, had not happened. A perfect balance between her heart and her head had resulted in a life undisturbed by the disappointments and betrayals or even the unfortunate accidents that had beset her contemporaries and had resulted in a trail of divorces, depressions and at least one fatherless child.

Attentions that Sybilla did not seek she nipped politely in the bud, while those she did seek but could not win she cast swiftly from her mind. Usually with a vigorous game of squash.

Twelve thousand miles away from the English suburb in which Sybilla's life was neatly located, Lionel McAlister had grown from boy to man on a prosperous sheep station near the township of Dunedin, on the South Island of New Zealand. The premature death of his father had thrust onto his robust shoulders a responsibility that might well have daunted an older man. But both Lionel and the acres he managed had flourished, albeit at the expense of his social life, until his bachelorhood, while not exactly confirmed, was certainly established. The girls he had grown up with had married and became unavailable. A few, for one reason or another, became available a second time but Lionel was not tempted. He'd had a fling or two when studying agriculture at college, and there were girls on whom he could rely to round off a good night on the town when he visited Wellington for the wool sales, but it was his passion for golf that absorbed the limited time he had for recreation. He played extremely well and, rather to his surprise, a month before his fortieth birthday, became South Island Amateur Champion, winning not only a prodigious silver trophy for his mother's sideboard but a two-week trip to the United Kingdom, where he was to be entertained at golfing shrines from Sunningdale to Saint Andrews, and fêted at a gala dinner at London's Dorchester Hotel. Everyone, even everyone in Dunedin, had heard of that. The arrangements were to be co-ordinated by the secretary of a golf club in Surrey, a position held at that time by—did you guess? Of course you did. By Sybilla.

She took charge of him at the airport, saw him through his jetlag and organised his itinerary with a cool competence that impressed him.

"She's hardly drop-dead gorgeous," he murmured to his shaving mirror after a couple of days in her company. "But you can have a laugh with her. She's a good mate. Even if she does sound like she's got a plum in her mouth."

Sybilla knew exactly what he should wear to the various celebrations he was to attend, and when formalities confused him, she guided him through them so that he was never patronised by the smooth, upper-class Brits who Lionel guessed were waiting for a chance to expose him as a gauche colonial. He rather enjoyed this dependence and encouraged Sybilla to show him the sights of London, which she did, from the Tower to Tate Modern.

Although Sybilla regretted that Lionel was not quite as tall as she—a disadvantage noticeable only when they danced together—and that being an antipodean, one did, sometimes, have to make allowances, she rather liked him. In fact, by the end of his two-week stay, she liked him a lot. She liked his voice, his broad shoulders and the way she was curiously and pleasantly affected by his direct gaze. She liked the way he was different from all the other men she had ever known. When he invited her to accompany him to the Dorchester dinner she spent an entire year's clothes' budget on one, stunning frock. No one had ever seen her looking so good, and with her at his side Lionel rose to his feet and addressed his hosts with an ease and an assurance that would have amazed the townsfolk of Dunedin. Relaxed by lavish hospitality he held her close as they danced, and in a rush of affection invited her to visit him in New Zealand as soon and for as long as she wished.

Later he was vaguely aware of tumbling into the reeking depths of a cab and of Sybilla's scented presence there with him. As they lurched into the traffic of Park Lane he enveloped her in a close embrace to which, after some time, he sensed a certain resistance on her part. Embarrassed, he persisted and they wrestled all the way to Hammersmith Broadway, Lionel giggling foolishly and Sybilla wearing an increasingly hard, fixed smile. Wherever upon her person Lionel placed an eager hand he encountered one of her hands. He could not believe how many hands, elbows and even knees she possessed, or how even this number could be simultaneously in quite so many places at once. By the time they reached his hotel he felt as he remembered feeling in the worst, greenest moments of his adolescence. Aroused and uncomfortable, he had been rebuffed. Worst of all he was aware that this was no ordinary girl who found him fresh and stupid. This was Sybilla. For whom he had respect. For whom, he realised suddenly, he cared. Mortified, he scrambled out of the cab, gave the driver a twenty-pound note and instructed him to take the lady home.

It was a long and lonely ride. Sybilla sat, resisting the motion of the cab and thinking seriously about herself and about Lionel, and then again about herself. Had she repelled him out of habit? Or was she incapable of responding as she wanted to respond? As she must respond if, tomorrow, Lionel was not going to vanish forever from her life. The taxi slowed and stopped at the gate of the neat little house in which, since the deaths of her parents, Sybilla had lived, alone.

Lionel had hoped she would not be at the airport but there she was, flicking a speck of dust from the lapel of his Dunedin Golf Club blazer and telling him she had some long-service leave due and asking whether he was serious about his invitation. What could he say? He did point out that it was winter in New Zealand and consequently a lousy time to visit the South Island, but Sybilla said she loved cold weather and was dying to wear the fake fur coat she'd recently bought in Harvey Nic's July sale. Confused and hungover, Lionel boarded his plane.

The best deal, Sybilla discovered from her travel agent, involved a stopover somewhere hot and tropical. Three weeks later she was sitting in the Hotel Frangipani's private minibus as it plunged through a humid darkness and at breathtaking and terrifying speed penetrated reeking suburbs. She was a little disappointed by the tacky modernity of the hotel but after fourteen hours on the plane wanted nothing more than a shower and a long sleep.

A lithe, golden-skinned porter carried her bags to the lift and into her room where he smiled—he had the whitest teeth—bowed and left her. She squeezed out onto the tiny balcony and peered down at the city. She had expected the air to be heavy with the scent of the jungle, and that she would watch a full moon rise from a tropical sea. But all she could smell was diesel fumes. The only sound was the throb of traffic.

It was astonishingly hot. She peeled off her sticky clothes and stood for a long time in the cramped shower cubicle, letting the tepid water pour over her. She was towelling her hair when she was startled by a discreet tap on her door, and disconcerted to realise that someone, unbidden, was entering her room. She snatched the nearest garment—

which happened to be the fake fur coat—and just managed to plunge her arms into it and gather it around her before her visitor came into view. It was the young porter. He stood, smiling his shy, white smile and balancing a small tray on the fingers of one dusky hand. On the tray, pearled with condensation, was a half bottle of champagne. Beside it lay a spray of creamy, headily scented, Frangipani blossoms.

"Wong," he said, introducing himself, bowing charmingly. At first Sybilla thought he meant "wrong" because she had not ordered champagne and doubted its inclusion in her package deal. But he was unloading his tray, uncorking the bottle in a most professional way and carefully pouring the wine, glancing at her as he did so as though her look of astonishment and her protestations were a familiar response. He stood, lithe, golden, smiling. And waited. "If only I could tip him he would go!" Sybilla thought desperately. But having been assured that "all gratuities were included in the price" she had no local currency. The fur of her coat prickled horribly, its nylon lining clammy against her drenched skin. Rivulets of perspiration were already trickling between her breasts. Sweat was stinging her eyes and dripping from her chin. If only he would go! But he continued to stand, a half-smile on his lips and a look—dark, velvety—was it slightly knowing? in his eyes.

"Surely there is something I can do for madam?" he coaxed, his voice as soft as his sidelong glance. "Something—madam—desires?"

Suddenly Sybilla understood! She remembered giggled reports from her women friends of "toy-boy room service" at exotic stopovers. Consternation was quickly followed by indignation and then by an almost irrepressible desire to laugh at her ludicrous situation! But Sybilla was no fool.

There *was* something she wanted—or at any rate needed—if she was to succeed with Lionel. And she did want, more than she had ever wanted anything before, to succeed with Lionel. She drained her champagne flute and returned her visitor's smile.

To begin with Sybilla found Mr Wong a little surprising. But as the velvety night passed she began, quite without realising it, to surprise Mr Wong.

Lionel waited uneasily at the airport. He had taken the precaution of booking two separate rooms for the one night they were to spend in Wellington. But as Sybilla's face lit with pleasure when she picked him out of the crowd his spirits rose. People looked at them—the well-heeled grazier greeting his cool, jet-setting lady.

In her hotel room Sybilla kicked off her shoes, smiled at Lionel and reclined in an uninhibited and most endearing way against the soft pillows of the bed. An hour later Lionel cancelled his reservation for the second room.

Next day, before they flew to Dunedin, Sybilla cashed a traveller's cheque, folded a fifty-dollar bill into an envelope and addressed it care of the Hotel Frangipani. "They looked after me so well, darling," she told Lionel. She was—and felt certain she always would be—deeply grateful to Mr Wong.

# The Taking of Aunt Orla

"The Taking of Aunt Orla" is part of an on-going project—a collection of five Irish stories.

Until the Christmas of my eighth year I thought all families were like mine. Well, not quite like, for I was the only child in our house and this, in the Catholic Ireland of the 1930s was in itself uncommon. To me it was not unusual when hushed conversation between my father and my mother was broken off when I entered our warm kitchen on my return from school, or from fetching kindling or throwing corn to the hens.

Sometimes my Uncle Michael would call in on his way home from selling the crabs and fish he caught in his little boat off the strand where my grandmother's cottage stood alone, a mile below the mountain to which our small-holding clung. Then there would be three voices hushed into silence when I burst in upon them.

I had other uncles who had gone, before I was old enough to remember them, across the sea to find work.

Then there was Aunt Orla, the youngest of Grandma's children, who lived with her where they had all been born, in the two-roomed cottage on the edge of the bay. Orla, with her pale skin and long, silky hair as black as pitch. I longed for hair like hers. For mine was red as a carrot and I hated it and the teasing it brought me at school.

Aunt Orla seldom spoke. Silently she would climb onto the swing that was suspended on long ropes from a great pine—the single tree on the edge of that desolate, shingle beach. Standing on its seat and reaching up with her arms, Aunt Orla would arch her body back and forth, swinging higher and higher until she seemed to touch the sky, the black hair and her wide skirt flying. And she would sing, leaving thin strands of sound floating in the air as she rose and fell. I wanted to try the swing but she would never let me.

"When you grow bigger, Bridie," my grandmother soothed, passing me a jam spoon to lick.

Early each December my mother made plum puddings and stood them, round and tightly wrapped in white linen, side by side, on the dresser, ready for Christmas. One for us, up at the croft, and another for grandmother, Uncle Michael and Aunt Orla.

That year, on a raw, midwinter afternoon, I ran the three miles home from school, my picture of the nativity stuffed inside my coat, to find Uncle Michael's van, pock-marked with rust, standing in the mud outside our gate. Wind snatched the smoke from our stumpy chimney and lamplight glimmered out through our windowpanes.

I paused outside the door, for the voices in the kitchen were raised, the wind and the roar of surf, pounding the strand a mile below, drowning the words. Yet odd phrases reached my ears. I heard my mother: "But it cannot go on!" Then Orla's name and Uncle Michael's voice: "We have no choice! Don't you see that?"

As I entered the kitchen Michael rose from the table, bade us goodbye and was gone. My mother turned her back on me and stirred the stew that was our supper. For a moment my daddy stared at the picture I had brought him. Then he lifted his head and in a low voice said, "And hasn't Michael forgot to take the pudden down the hill!"

We ate in silence that Christmas Eve, for no carollers ever came to sing at our wind-wracked door. I hung my stocking on my bedpost, prayed as usual to Our Lady for a brother

26

or a sister, and with the uproar of the gale in my ears, slept.

Hours later, my room lit by a low moon, I unpacked my stocking. There was an orange. A toothbrush. A pair of mittens knitted by my mother. A packet of wine gums and a purse with half a crown in it. I knew my best present lay under the small tree, which, while I slept, my parents would have decorated with familiar tinsels and stars. I crept through into the still-warm kitchen, held the wrapped parcel to my ear, shook it, guessed what it contained, but I knew I must not open it.

The wind had dropped. I could hear the slow-breaking waves, which, in the wake of the storm, dropped onto the shingle way below. It was not morning yet. Too early to begin Christmas. But there was grandmother's pudding, still on our dresser. I pulled on my coat and my boots and with the pudding clasped to my chest, opened the back door and stepped out into solid cloud, luminous with moonlight.

Every stone and twist of that steep path, a shortcut to my grandmother's place, was familiar to me, so that my descent, blindfolded by the mist, was thrilling. When I reached the velvety turf that surrounded her cottage, I was breathless and laughing aloud.

I remembered, afterwards, that the swing was moving. Back and forth, as though someone had just that moment slid from the seat, leaving it in motion. But no one was there. The back door stood open. This was odd, so early on a cold morning. I stepped inside and stood in the silent, low-ceilinged kitchen. A chair lay overturned near the scrubbed table. The door to the second room, where my grandmother and Aunt Orla slept, was open. On the far side of the kitchen was a curtained alcove in which my Uncle Michael's bed stood. I could see his blankets, pushed aside as though he

27

had risen hurriedly. There was no sound other than the slow boom of the surf on the strand and the ticking of the clock. I called out for my grandmother and from the bedroom a small sound reached me.

I found her on the floor in the space between the bed and the wall. I thought at first that she was ill, until I saw the knife and the cuts across her poor face and down her old arms. There was blood on the bedding.

It was then that I heard my Aunt Orla. She was out in the yard and she was singing. I pulled aside the window curtain and there she was, just visible in the thinning mist, standing on the seat of the swing, her arms reaching up and twisted through the ropes. Arching her back and then leaning forward, she swung higher and higher, the mist wreathing round her like smoke. And she was bare. Naked as the day. White skin shining. Black hair flowing like silk from her head and curling densely at her groin. I dropped the curtain and turned my attention to my grandmother, dabbing at her wounds and urging her back onto the bed where I could care for her. But she shook her head.

"Go, Bridie! Run home! Quickly! Before she comes again!"

But I would not go and pulled the covers from the bed and tucked them around my poor grandmother where she lay. We heard the kitchen door crash open and the sound of Orla's bare feet slapping across the stone floor and her voice, calling, demanding an answer. My grandmother drew me down close to her, pulled the blanket over me and held me tightly. Orla came into the bedroom, prowling, searching, shouting. It seemed that at any moment she would discover us.

Then we heard the sound of my Uncle Michael's truck

approaching down the mountain. Orla heard it too and fled. There were voices in the yard, voices I did not recognise. Hidden by the curtain I peered out.

Orla was back on the swing. There was a van behind Michael's truck and some men from the Garda were spreading out, surrounding the outbuildings. Others, in white coats, approached my aunt. She was laughing, swinging higher and higher. As they closed on her she kicked out, trying to keep them off her. But they caught her at last by her long, bare legs and dragged her from the swing, forcing her arms into a white jacket and binding its long sleeves tight against her while she screamed and screamed.

In my childish confusion I thought the men might take me too. I climbed out through the window and fled. Grandmother had tried to hide me. Now I must hide myself. I squeezed through a familiar gap in the planking at the rear of the boat shed where my Uncle Michael kept his nets and crab pots, thinking that no one would come there. But the Garda were there before me! I crouched in the shadows, hardly daring to breathe.

Intent on their own business the Garda did not see me. Soon I understood that they had found what they were searching for.

A disused canvas sail, long since replaced on my uncle's boat by an outboard motor, had, for as far back as my memory stretched, been stowed, rolled up and suspended across the rafters overhead. This now lay on the earthen floor. Something was exposed among the rotting canvas folds. At first I barely recognised the confused shape as the body of a man. I glimpsed his blanched and hollowed face and the bones that were his hands. The pale shirt was in tatters and marked with dark stains. My Uncle Michael was sitting on a upturned barrel, his head was in his hands, his voice was muffled.

"Yes, I knew," he said. "We all knew. But the fault was his! He lied to her! Orla was…delicate. Something broke in her head on that day he said he would come to her no more. And when he told her why—that he already had a wife…and children…she flew at him and cut him. Slashed him with our mother's kitchen knife." My uncle paused, lost in the memory of it, the Garda watching. "You would have thought such violence would have killed the child she carried. But no. It came soon after."

They took them in for questioning. Uncle Michael and my daddy. Three days they were away. Then they came home. But Aunt Orla never did come home.

The family's silence closed over her like a bog pool over a pebble. We kept, as usual, to ourselves. Aunt Orla's absence was never discussed in our kitchen, nor in my grandmother's.

I was sent to school in Belfast where I lodged with mother's cousin. I grew. My freckles faded, my hair darkened to auburn and I learned the ways of the world. But my mind still looped back to what had happened on the Christmas Day of my eighth year. Over and over I examined the half-remembered words and vaguely recollected scenes, picking through them, trying them this way and that as though piecing together a jigsaw more puzzling than the one I had been given that Christmas, and which, guided by the gaudy picture on its lid, I had completed during those curious, silent days after Aunt Orla was taken. I recalled, for instance, other occasions, when my father and my mother suffered injuries and had explained them away, saying they had been caused by a glancing blade, a badly managed scythe, a vicious dog.

And grandmother, bruised. Uncle Michael, cut across the cheek.

But it was years before I interpreted the most startling thing I had seen that Christmas morning. It was the mass of dusty hair clinging to the skull of the man whose body lay wrapped in the sail. The sight of it lingered, nudging my mind. For it was the same, harsh, red-colour as my own had been.

And so it was that one day, like a blow under the ribs, Michael's words that morning in the boat shed made sense to me. I knew why it was that Our Lady had ignored my prayers for a second and perhaps a third child to be born in our house. It was because there had not been a first! The woman who had mothered me and the man who raised me were not my parents! Orla, mad and locked away, had carried me! To protect her, the brothers had hoisted the body of my flame-haired father up onto the boat house rafters, below which, for years, our family came and went while the guilt of it sighed like the quiet waves on the shingle or throbbed like a fetid wound when gales blew and surf pounded. Until the moment was reached, the moment that had to be reached, when, that Christmas morning, our secret could no longer be kept.

# The Mourner

"The Mourner" was one of five stories with the umbrella title *Easter*. It was transmitted in March 2002 and produced by Sara Davies, BBC Bristol.

The sun had risen from behind the dark mass of the presbytery and its light, piercing stained glass, was daubing the interior of the church with colour.

Muriel was about to perform a similar function. In her case the colour took the form of the floral arrangements at the pulpit steps, beside the font and on the altar itself, for which she was responsible.

March was a difficult month but today Muriel's task would be made easier by one bunch of white narcissi and another of blue irises, which someone had kindly left in the church porch. These would provide a useful contrast to the prevailing yellowness of the daffodils Muriel had picked from her own garden. She was not fond of daffodils, which she considered strident and overpowering. She tried, in her arrangements, to soften their effect with sprays of pussy willow.

She nodded good morning to the saints and the apostles above her, filled her jug with water from the tap in the utility room next to the vestry, carried it through into the body of the church, and under the bland gazes of Saints Peter and Paul began topping up the water in various vases.

A cleaner had that morning polished the pews. The lavender scent of her duster lingered, dispelling an underlying reek of dampness.

Absorbed by her task, Muriel carefully inserted the irises between the delicate narcissi, while sparrows quarrelled among the gargoyles, and pigeons argued in the churchyard trees.

She paused, appraising her work, and heard footsteps. Someone had entered the church. Muriel was not an unduly nervous woman but considered it wise, if you were to be alone in a building with someone, to satisfy yourself that that person intended you no mischief.

The elderly man was neatly dressed. As she watched, he removed his homburg hat, sidled into a pew, dropped to his knees and bent his head in prayer. A shaft of sunlight, which had assumed a greenish tinge as it passed through a stained glass representation of Saint George engaged by the dragon, tinted the man's grey hair and bleached the colour from his bony fingers.

Muriel, clearly in no danger from this visitor, continued her work and had almost forgotten his presence when he appeared unexpectedly in the tail of her eye. She turned, saw the sheaf of lilies in the crook of his arm and for a moment wondered if he intended to donate them to the church. His first words, however, dispelled any such idea.

"For her grave," he said, as though sensing Muriel's hopes for the lilies. "My wife's. It's the anniversary you see. Twelve months to the day. You were here then, too. Seeing to the flowers."

"Was I?" said Muriel, her eyes on his cellophane-shrouded offering.

"She told me not to bring flowers. She was convinced that death was the end, you see."

Muriel expressed regret, intending to convey not only her sympathy for the man in his bereavement but her concern regarding his wife's lack of faith.

"And so did I," he announced, glancing keenly at Muriel. "Then!"

"Then?" Muriel echoed.

The man continued. "You, I imagine, are a believer?" Muriel said she was. He drew close to her. "But can you, I wonder, remember precisely when and by what means you were convinced?" He stared intently into her eyes. "I *can*, you see!" His face was lit by a curious zeal. "It was in this very place! Twelve months ago! To the hour!"

Muriel felt slightly uneasy. It would be at least ten minutes before vicar and verger would arrive to conduct this morning's funeral service. Muriel still had to check on the flowers at the base of the font, but as a Christian and a servant of the church, it was clearly her duty to be sympathetic to this grieving convert. To listen to him and be supportive. But it had to be admitted, his manner was beginning to concern her.

He trotted beside her as she headed back, through the vestry to refill the water jug. The door of the utility room stood open to the morning. Across the churchyard, against a sombre screen of yew, was a pile of earth, spoil from the grave that was to be filled that day. Near this a plain marble cross glittered in harsh sunlight.

"My wife's," the man said, pointing.

He followed Muriel back through the church and stood beside her at the font. With his bunch of lilies held tightly in his hand he gathered himself to speak.

"She was extremely fond of her cats," he began. This seemed to Muriel to be an unexpected start to a story of conversion, but she concealed her surprise and began extracting from the brass vase at the base of the font several daffodils that were past their best. "Three, she had," the man continued. "Faith, Hope and Charity their names were." Muriel smiled indulgently. "Poor Charity was run over and Hope died suddenly three weeks after my wife. So I was left with Faith. Except, of course, that at that time I was without it. I mean," he muttered, embarrassed by his confusion, "that I had the cat but not the faith, if you understand me."

Muriel said she thought she did and began to look forward to the arrival of the vicar, which would put an end, once and for all, to the ramblings of this sad and possibly mildly deranged person.

"But it wasn't Faith. Not the cat, I mean, that gave me the proof!"

"No?" said Muriel.

"No. Because it was here, you see!"

"The cat was here?"

"No! The proof! Not the cat! Leastways not *my* cat. Not Faith!"

Muriel stared at him. He was becoming flushed. Beads of perspiration on his forehead glittered strangely with the colours from the stained glass above their heads. The lilies trembled inside their creaking cellophane.

"But there was a cat here!" His excitement, if possible, was increasing as his recollection of the event flooded back to him. "A black cat," he continued, pleased to see that Muriel was now paying proper attention to him. "It was just inside the lychgate when I first noticed it. Stalking along behind the pall-bearers. Then it followed them into the church! Bold as brass! Down the aisle! Very dignified. Tail straight as a needle. Just the tip twitching. You know the way they do…"

Muriel did know. She had forgotten about her flower arrangement and was standing, her mouth ajar, a splash of vermilion, by courtesy of Judas Iscariot's cloak, disguising her pallor.

"It sat down," the man continued. "Didn't stir all through the service! And when the coffin was carried out to the grave the cat followed!" He scanned Muriel's incredulous face. "It's true!" he said. "And afterwards, as I left the churchyard, I looked across and it was sitting there, at the grave-side, looking at me! Bold as brass! Such green eyes! I can see them now!"

"Where?" Muriel asked, rather sharply, peering anxiously into the shadows. The man ignored her.

"I knew, of course, what it was," he said and then, aware of Muriel's reaction, added, "don't be alarmed, my dear! It was nothing sinister. Simply my wife's way of letting me know that her spirit still exists! Is watching over me! That there is a hereafter!"

Muriel began to feel quite light-headed.

"The revelation has changed my life!" he continued, happily, then he paused, surprised by Muriel's increasing tension. "You seem upset!"

He waited, obviously expecting an explanation, while she tried desperately to think of one. There was one, of course, but not one she could possibly give to the man into whose puzzled, watery eyes she found herself gazing.

"It's nothing," she began, wracking her brain. "But…there is to be a funeral. In ten minutes. Here. This morning!"

"I should enjoy that!" the man said, easily. "I'll sit at the back! They won't even know I'm here!"

"No! You mustn't!" Muriel's shrill voice smacked against the walls and echoed from the fan vaulting. The stone faces of the saints showed surprise and the Archangel Gabriel glanced sharply down.

Having always regarded untruths as a poor way out of unpleasantness, Muriel was an unpractised liar. She raised her eyes to the various disciples by whom she was surrounded. "It's to be a very private funeral!" she said desperately, and for no reason she could think of. She braced herself for the inevitable questions, and did not know how she would answer them.

Then, quite suddenly, laid out before her, immaculate and complete, a lily in its hand, was a perfect and beautiful lie. Placed there, Muriel was certain, by a divine power. She leaned towards the man and whispered one word. "Royalty!"

Surprised, he glanced round at the quite ordinary church, its doors wide, its run-of-the-mill flowers, predominantly daffodils of the most common, bright yellow kind, and had opened his mouth to speak when Muriel put a finger to her lips.

"I mustn't say any more," Muriel whispered. "The tightest security is in place. Any breach could put lives in danger. Where royalty is concerned the utmost care must be taken in these dangerous times."

Muriel inclined her head, so convinced by her lie that she could almost see the armour-plated limousine nosing through the country lanes towards the church and the armed bodyguards, lurking near the lychgate.

"Royalty?" the man breathed.

Muriel nodded. "So perhaps if you could leave? Now? It would be best. Safest. Don't you think? We don't want…" she paused, "…any unpleasantness, do we?"

He blinked, nodded and glanced nervously out through the open door.

The first arrivals were at that moment parking their cars. The beetle-black roof of the hearse was just visible above an horizon of clipped privet. Vicar and verger were progressing across from the presbytery.

"Go!" said Muriel, to the man. "Quickly! Through the vestry! There's a gate at the far side of the churchyard. You could visit your wife's grave on your way. I do hate to hurry you but..." She watched him go, glanced up at the Archangel Gabriel, who seemed now to wish to have nothing whatsoever to do with the situation.

Moments later and still shaken, Muriel seated herself breathlessly in a pew near the back of the church as the first of the few mourners followed their shadows into the church porch.

The service began. As the pall-bearers carried the coffin down the long aisle, past Muriel's flowers at font and pulpit, they were followed, at a respectful distance, by a lean black cat. It stepped elegantly forward, tail erect, and sat stock still, throughout the brief ceremony, blinking in a pool of sunlight that spread the colours of stained glass over the engraved stones with which the aisle was paved. "Here lyeth. Here lyeth..."

"Oh, look! A pussy-cat!" whispered a woman who had seated herself beside Muriel.

"It always comes," Muriel murmured. "Never misses. It will follow the coffin to the graveside. You'll see."

And it did. Stepping carefully through the wet grass, shaking the dew from its paws and sitting primly while ashes went to ashes and dust to dust. There was an anxious moment when Muriel wondered whether the man, tempted by the prospect of a glimpse of a royal mourner, might have given way to his curiosity and concealed himself somewhere in the churchyard. But the lilies were lying on his wife's grave and there was no sign of him. Those attending withdrew, leaving the cat to maintain its sleek, solitary vigil.

Muriel continued with her floral duties and for some time

was sustained by a conviction that her lie, justified by a desire to preserve the man's newly acquired faith, had been both inspired and condoned by the saints themselves. Until one morning, when it occurred to her that the devil too was represented above her.

From that moment, serpent, dragon and Lucifer himself appeared to be regarding her as a fellow-conspirator, leering down at her while the eyes of the carved angels and glazed disciples were so loaded with pious disapproval that Muriel could no longer meet them, and her duties in the church gave her no pleasure at all.

Within months she had relinquished responsibility for the flowers and was dedicating her resulting free time to voluntary work in a local charity shop. She reduced her church-going to the services at Easter and at Christmas, when she would keep her eyes on her hymnbook or on the stone paving of the aisle, though even these could embarrass her with their incised inscriptions, "Here lyeth," "Here lyeth."

# Sea Change

"Sea Change" was transmitted in June 1997. It was produced in Bristol by Viv Beeby and read by June Barrie.

The cliff, as they sailed towards it, appeared impenetrable. A mass of rock tilting down, plunging into deep water. Yet there it was, clearly marked on their chart, an inlet, the single break in a long stretch of coastline.

It had taken them three weeks to sail their small yacht through the islands, from Greece, to Turkey. The April weather had initially been foul. Cold rains and adverse winds had hindered them. Twice they had been hit by sudden storms that had laid them on their beam and forced them, under storm jib and reefed mainsail, to run for cover and lie among sheltering caiques in small harbours and anchorages. But since they had rounded Cape Cnuidos the winds had eased and grown warm, the twilights were violet and mild. Now, relaxed and rested, they forgot the anxieties of the early days of the voyage and dawdled along, close to the breathtaking coastline. They had seen no one for days. Only the occasional clamour of goat bells, borne on the warm breeze, suggested the presence of herdsmen, scratching a living from the mountainous land that was slipping past the boat's port bow, while the horizon merged imperceptibly with a pale sky.

As their voyage had absorbed their attention, first focussing and then draining their energies, they had entered an altered state. Suffered a sea change. Now, within easy reach of their destination, they were relaxed, drowsy. Day followed day. They drifted in their own space, their own time.

A soldier's wind had, that morning, drawn them eastwards

along the southern Turkish coast and in an hour or so, had the breeze continued, they would have reached Marmaris, but at midday they were suddenly becalmed, the surface of the sea flattening under the beat of the sun, their boat wallowing on the swell. They knew there would be no wind before late afternoon, so an hour or two at anchor in a quiet cove was tempting.

"Still can't see it," said the man, re-checking his chart. The woman leaned over his shoulder, her finger marking the place on the chart where the inlet was shown.

"Should be dead ahead," she said.

The man went for'ard, leaned on the pulpit and screwed up his eyes against the glare. Still the rocky shore appeared unbroken, blank and solid. Indigo blue water beneath the hull confirmed the reading on his depth gauge. They had a good four fathoms under them and could risk creeping in, sails flapping, for another hundred yards or so.

Then he saw it. A narrow gap between two colossal slabs of rock. Beyond these the inlet widened. Enclosed water, flanked by steep, pine-clad cliffs, glimmered, turquoise and still.

They stood off, lowered their sails, prepared the anchor chain, started the engine and, while the woman kept watch for submerged rocks, the man eased his boat carefully forward.

Once through the narrow entrance they found themselves in a circular cove. The man lowered the kedge, watching its descent through water so clear that he could see the wisp of sand that lifted as it struck the seabed. He laid out the chain and signalled to the woman to cut the engine. The silence that dropped over them was like the spell of an enchanter.

While the man drew the cork on the last but one bottle of the wine they had bought in Samos, the woman diced feta cheese, laid it on a bed of sliced tomato, loaded it with handfuls of black olives, drenched it in oil, garnished it with pepper and cut thick slices from their last loaf of coarse, dry bread.

After their meal they made love under the hot sun and lay, sleepy, in the heat, while the little boat swung quietly at anchor, her shadow creeping this way and that, over the white pebbles three fathoms beneath her keel.

At last the man got to his feet and dived neatly off the stern. The woman peered down through the fractured surface, watching his skin take on a pale and then deeper greenish blue tone as he swam down towards the seabed. Then he turned, kicked up towards her and broke the surface explosively, gasping with the shock of the cold water on his sunburned skin. She followed, striking out ahead of him, eager to reach the warmer shallows.

They splashed ashore and over the hot shingle to a patch of close-cropped grass where cyclamen grew. All round them the aromatic cliffs rose, cupping warm air resonant with the humming of bees. They lay in the sun, the drying salt prickling and tightening on their bare skin.

"I have a sensation," said the man, looking out, past their boat, through the gap in the rock, "that nothing exists beyond this place. Our home, our work, friends, responsibilities… . All gone…"

"I wish it was true," she said, spreading her limbs on the warm grass. "I wish this was all there was, all there ever will be! We could make a libation to the appropriate god… . Along with a request that the rest of our lives be put on hold."

"To Poseidon, perhaps?" the man suggested, drowsily. "He's

looked after us pretty well these last few weeks." Then he raised his voice, pitching his question into a silence that absorbed it instantly. "Did you hear that, master?" They smiled. The man inhaled, tasting the scent of resin, thyme and lavender in the air, then rolled onto his back, opened his eyes and allowed his mind to fill with the blue of the sky. A small white cloud was moving, quite fast across it. At once the tension was back.

"Time to move," he said, getting to his feet and pulling the woman up beside him. She too had seen the cloud.

It was when they reached the water's edge that they heard the laughter. It began as a chuckle, low and mischievous. Then it grew, encircling them. Peel after peel of bellowing mirth. Instantly their nakedness embarrassed them. The woman lowered herself quickly into the shallows and lunged forward, swimming fast. The man, close behind her, followed, head down, kicking hard towards their boat, making a dozen strong strokes before lifting his head to breathe. The woman was treading water beside him, her expression incredulous.

"It's not there!" she shouted, her voice shrill with alarm. "Where is it?"

Their boat was gone. Where, moments before, it had been rocking quietly at anchor, now there was nothing but the unbroken surface of the inlet. Frantically they scanned every inch of the small, enclosed space while the laughter continued, amplified by the surrounding rock, ricocheting, howling, assaulting them from all sides while they floundered pointlessly, towards the centre of the cove, the place where the boat had been. They swam in circles, turning this way and that in panic. Small waves slapped into their faces, blinding them with spray.

"Shut up!" the man yelled at the echoing cliffs, his voice thin and desperate. "Shut up!"

The appalling laughter died abruptly and, as suddenly, they saw their boat, its white hull gleaming, the steel ladder, which gave access to the stern, only feet from them. The woman hauled herself aboard while the man, one hand gripping the ladder rail, looked back, scanning the dense undergrowth.

A rising wind was stirring the leaves of the creepers and shrubs that festooned the cliffs. But there was no sign of human movement, no dark eyes, peering, no cacophony of goat bells to confirm the presence of a herdsman. Only the innocent rasp of wind in the crowns of the tallest pines.

Without a word the woman scrambled to the foredeck, where, hand over hand, she retrieved the anchor faster than she had ever done before. The man started the engine and, when the kedge was clear of the water, opened the throttle. The boat moved forward, gathering speed as they approached the fissure in the rock. The wind, which now funnelled through it, struck, cold, on their wet skin, and the gap in the cliffs seemed narrower than when they had entered the cove. Looming rock appeared to be closing on them. With inches to spare and the sound of the engine hammering between the two cliff faces, the man took his boat through, exhaling with relief as they emerged into open sea. They were out. Pitching and slamming in the disturbed, exposed water—but out.

While the woman struggled to stow the anchor chain and secure the kedge, the man maintained his course until they were well clear of the shore. When the woman came aft, took the helm and held the boat bow-on to the wind, the man ran for'ard, and leaving the mainsail furled set the Genoa, returning to the cockpit to winch in the flogging sail. He took the helm and brought the little craft beam-on to the wind. As the Genoa filled and began to pull, the motion of the boat changed, steadying under the influence of the sail, and they surged forward, riding the swell. He cut the engine. The sea slipped, hissing, under their hull.

"Go below and get warm," he said to the woman.

From the shelter of the cabin, as she wrapped herself in a towel, she said, "What idiots we are!" They laughed, partly with relief at having successfully negotiated the difficult exit from the cove but, mostly, to cover their panic at the apparent loss of their boat. But, as she towelled her hair, the woman's face clouded.

"But someone was there," she said. "And the boat wasn't!"

"She must have been," he said, looking ahead now, picking out landmarks and relating them to his course. "Trick of the light. She was in shadow, bow-on to us. With the sun in our eyes and the wind picking up the spray, we missed her."

"We didn't! You know we didn't." The woman shoved her arms into the sleeves of her sweater. "She wasn't there. And then she was!"

"Too much wine with lunch, perhaps. A timely warning about our drinking habits!" The woman smiled reluctantly. "Stick the kettle on, love," he said to her, steering the conversation away from the incident in the cove. "Then take the helm while I get some clothes on."

Two hours later they were on the town quay at Marmaris, moored up to a converted Baltic trader whose master had taken their warps, helped them make fast their boat and introduced himself as Andreis.

The man had sailed from Holland years previously and was now living aboard his boat, moving at whim, from one Aegean anchorage to another. In good English and with phraseology and an accent just strong enough to establish his Dutch origins, he invited them to share his meal that evening.

As darkness fell they descended into the lamplight of his warm, timbered saloon and offered him the last of their Samoan wine.

"Quite a blow this afternoon!" the Dutchman said later, refilling the man's glass. "Coming from the west, you would have had to run before it. Must have been quite a ride!"

"We came out of a cove into the teeth of it!" said the woman and, proud of her seamanship added: "A Genoa run, all the way in to Marmaris."

"Cove?" enquired the Dutchman, draining the bottle.

"Yeah," said the man. "About ten miles west of here. We were becalmed this morning and dropped anchor there for an hour or so."

The Dutchman shook his head. "There is no longer any cove ten miles west from here," he said, puzzled.

"Easy enough to miss," said the man. "The entrance is narrow and almost invisible from the sea."

"I know the place," said their host. "I have anchored there many times myself, you see. A circular inlet with steep cliff all around, ya?"

"That's the one!" said the woman. "We had lunch there. And swam. We thought we were alone and were embarrassed by a Turkish peeping Tom!" She was about to tell him how they had, for several anxious moments, thought their boat had dragged its anchor. But something in the Dutchman's face made her hesitate.

"But this is not possible," he said.

"Why?"

"Because five years ago there was a 'quake here. Four

point five on the Richter scale. It did very little damage. A few dwellings collapsed up in the mountains behind the town, that was all. But it caused a…how do you say it?…a rock-slide, ya? The entrance to that cove was quite closed up." He looked at their incredulous faces. "This is most strange. But you must believe me. I know this coast intimately. There is no other place you could have confused it with. Ask any of the boatmen on the quay. They will tell you. That cove is gone. Filled in when the cliff slipped. And there is no other." He paused, embarrassed at having exposed their faulty navigation, then reached into a locker. "And now you should have brandy," he added, smiling at their blank faces. "I think you need it!"

Later, boarding their own boat, they paused to check their mooring lines and then sat in the cockpit, side by side in the cold darkness.

"We *were* there," the woman whispered, knowing where the man's thoughts lay. "We even wished we need never leave it."

Beside her he dropped his head into his hands. "Then the laughter," he said. "The laughter."

"Where would we be now," she asked, after some time, "if our wish had been granted?"

They began to feel a land breeze, flowing out from the town, bringing with it the scent of aromatic food cooking in the hot kitchens of tavernas noisy with music. Human voices rose and fell.

One by one the lights went out along the quay. Tomorrow, rational, sceptical even, they would accept a logical explanation of what had happened that day. But for what was left of the chill, starlit night, they remained haunted by her question, taking it wordlessly with them into their warm bunk and on into their sleep.

## Object of Desire

"Object of Desire" was recorded by the BBC in London and transmitted in the summer of 1998. The producer was Viv Beeby and the reader was Penelope Wilton.

Jennifer had been unaware of the effect she had on Noel Sloane. How could she know that she was the cause of the bright eyes, sharp mind and buoyant manner that he displayed when in her presence? She did not know that her new colleagues, men and women who had been acquainted with him for years, regarded him as somewhat sullen, dull and humourless.

The fact was that the moment he first set his eyes on her his life had been irrevocably changed. She struck such a chord in him that whenever he glimpsed her through the glass partitions of the open-plan offices, or observed her, loading her lunch tray in the canteen, or walking purposefully across the staff parking lot, her umbrella angled against the autumn rain, his pulse would race, he would lift his chin, adjust his tie and square his shoulders. The sight of her transformed his monochrome world into brilliant Technicolor. His dreams were altered, his ambitions shifted and his sense of responsibility dissolved into thin air.

Jennifer's recent appointment, as PA to the Chief Environment Officer at her local council offices, meant that she worked with Noel on several assignments during an average week. Sometimes they would be required to carry out a site visit together, or to discuss building proposals with a property developer. Then there were the weekly interdepartmental meetings. Noel cherished these. Cherished the hours when he could sit in close proximity to Jennifer, fetch her coffee, adjust the ventilation, retrieve the fallen pen.

He became consumed with desire for her. All previous

passions, including the cooling one that he was experiencing with his wife of twelve years, paled beside his feelings for Jennifer, whose wedding ring, he chose to believe, represented nothing more significant to her than his did to him. He was wrong. Her initial passion for her husband had matured into a mutually enjoyed fondness from which she was not inclined to stray.

Recently, when her two, amiable children became sufficiently independent, she had resumed her modest career in local government. Life, for her, was good. Had never, in fact, seemed better. Noel Sloane, into whose company she was frequently thrown, was both pleasant and amusing. She spoke of him to her husband and was planning to invite him and his wife to dinner when, quite unexpectedly, Noel pinned her against a site engineer's hut and blurted out his feelings for her. Initially embarrassed, she had laughed at him. Then, comprehending the intensity of his emotions, she pulled away and gently, firmly, coolly, told him that if he thought he had read any signs in her that she was interested in him, or indeed anyone other than her husband, he was mistaken.

Noel had backed away from her, turned on his heel, walked quickly to the departmental car and driven off at speed, leaving Jennifer to beg, from a mildly astonished contractor, a lift back to the council offices.

That began a series of weeks in which Noel watched her. Across the canteen, through the glass partitions, from the double-glazed windows as she parked her car, she felt his eyes upon her. Accusing. Pleading. His gaze loaded with unreasonable reproach. She contrived to adjust her work schedule so that their paths seldom crossed and the site visits fell to another member of staff. At departmental meetings she took care to arrive with a gaggle of women colleagues with whom she would sit in safety, avoiding eye contact with Noel. He began confronting her as she moved from one office to another, standing solidly in her path, his gaze heavy with dumb appeal, until, breathing an apology, she would sidle past him. Once, as she waited for the lift, he asked whether she had told her husband of their affair.

"No, of course not!" she said dismissively, realising, too late, that she had allowed herself to be trapped into confirming a level of conspiracy between the two of them. His thin smile, as she stepped briskly into the lift, was almost smug.

Flowers arrived on her desk. Freesias. Tuber roses. Lilies. Then, on her birthday, a lavish box of Belgian chocolates. She did not take the flowers home and pushed the chocolates, unopened, to the back of the drawer in her desk.

One wet Friday evening as she ran through rain to her car, she found him standing, gaunt and drenched, beside it. Half visible in the November dusk, he loomed towards her, his face distorted with an intensity of grief that alarmed her. She pushed past him, slammed the car door, reversed clumsily out of her parking space and, tyres skidding on the wet tarmac, accelerated away. Through her driving mirror she saw him turn, saw the clenched face blur into shadow.

She drove home fast and carefully, her headlights flicking past the autumn hedges, but she was unable to shake off a sense of unease, which persisted through the evening, spoiling her pleasure in the familiar family routine.

Her husband, assuming that she was, perhaps over-doing things, took her on a short winter break to Madeira, where he cosseted and soothed her, making practised and affectionate love to her until, removed from the cause of her tension, she relaxed, Noel Sloane's problems, his existence even, fading into insignificance.

On her first morning back at work, rested and lightly tanned, Jennifer was relieved to discover that her admirer was not lurking, eyes accusing, shoulders drooping, in the parking lot or near the lift.

She had barely put her handbag in her desk drawer before an excited office junior enquired whether she'd heard the news about Mr Sloane, and, discovering that she had not, delivered the facts. Noel, it seemed, had vanished. On the evening of the day that Jennifer had begun her holiday, he had left his house, ostensibly to fill his car with petrol. When several hours had passed and he had failed to return, his anxious wife had telephoned the local hospital and then the police station. Assuming there had been a domestic altercation, the police at first showed little interest, but now that eight days had passed since the disappearance and nothing had been seen or heard of Noel Sloane in all that time, they had begun to take the case more seriously, and after questioning his stricken wife and his mute children were making enquiries into his social life, and interviewing his colleagues at the council offices.

On the ninth day his car was found, concealed in scrub above some cliffs favoured by those determined on self-destruction, from below which the tide was known to bear its victims down the coast, depositing them, more often than not, on salt marshes thirty miles away.

Jennifer concealed her feelings when she heard this news, but the unpleasant sensation it provoked increased in intensity as the day passed. She pictured the corpse drifting in the shallow channels of the marsh and then splayed, beached and waterlogged, gilded with a deposit of fine silt. She longed to call her husband, tell him the whole story and receive from him the understanding support that she knew she deserved. But would he believe that she had never, at any point or in any way, encouraged Noel's attentions? Did she herself believe it? If only she had taken home the flowers and the chocolates, confided, then, her anxieties about Noel's attentions. Had she done so she could have relied on her husband's sympathy. But to tell him now? Had she, she wondered, been entirely honest with herself? Was she, on the one or two occasions when she and Noel had, in the course of their work, lunched together, a touch flirtatious? He had, to begin with, amused her. He had flattered her and made her feel attractive. But had she not, the instant his feelings were revealed to her, been scrupulous in ending the relationship? Even rearranging her assignments in order to avoid him?

She recalled the night in the car park, when he had appeared so stricken. So wrecked. And it was she who had wrecked him. She was, however inadvertently, the cause of the misery his wife was enduring, the loss his children were suffering.

Days passed. She was unable to sleep, frequently stealing downstairs in the small hours to do the ironing or some other silent, domestic chore to pass the time. When the headaches began she made an appointment with her GP, and embarrassed him by bursting into uncontrollable tears.

The pills helped. One to be taken three times a day, avoiding alcohol. She slept better and the headaches stopped. She obeyed the rules and restricted herself to soft drinks.

Christmas approached. At the office party the Director of Services spoke solemnly of Noel Sloane. A collection was taken up for the wife and children who continued to exist in an increasingly hopeless limbo. Jennifer, suddenly overtaken by a deep depression, accepted a glass or two of champagne before excusing herself and driving home.

The night was cold. A sharp frost sparkled on the grass verges. Icicles hung in the hedges and from the bare branches of the trees. The road was a familiar one. The drive home, routine, requiring little concentration, leaving her mind free. She felt suddenly angry. Angry with Noel for doing this outrageous thing to his wife, to his children, to Jennifer herself, for suicide was increasingly regarded as the only possible explanation for his disappearance. Why, when she was innocent, should she be made to feel so guilty? For she *was* innocent! She was not responsible for the fact that he had become besotted with her! She rounded a bend, slowing carefully in case there should be black ice on the road— and resolved to take charge of her imagination. She would exclude him from her mind. From this moment, whenever thoughts of him intruded, she would distract herself from the subject of Noel Sloane.

She began to relax. She felt calm. Powerful. Suddenly optimistic. The road unwound smoothly before her. The car surged on, through a fast, right-hand bend. Then up, over a rise.

He materialised suddenly from shadow into the white blaze of her headlights. The remembered stance, the pale, familiar face, his hand raised, extended towards her in a gesture of appeal. Noel! Directly in the path of her speeding car! She had destroyed him once, instinctively she avoided doing so again. Tramping on the brake pedal, she hauled the car round, away from him, felt the tyres lose traction, the wheel snatch violently from her hands. She spun once, twice…and slammed into an oak tree.

At the inquest the hitchhiker described the dark night, the icy road. He told the hushed court how, in the silence, he had heard the whine of a fast approaching vehicle and had turned to face it, arm extended, thumb raised, asking for a ride. Then, judging the car's speed to be too great to hope that it might stop for him, he had stepped back, pressing himself against the frosted hedge.

"She just lost it," he muttered, still shaken by the grisly sequence of events.

"Speak up," said the coroner.

"Lost it," he repeated, raising his voice. "There was no need for her to swerve."

On Christmas Eve, with the neighbourhood still stunned by the tragedy of Jennifer's death, Noel Sloane slid his key into the latch of his front door and walked back into his life. As his wife stared speechlessly at him, he said that he believed he had suffered some sort of breakdown, for he had no memory of where he had been. Later he was able to recall walking on the Yorkshire Moors, where he had come to himself and made his way home. After a suitable period of sick leave he resumed his work at the council offices.

Summing up, the coroner had attributed Jennifer's death to misadventure, describing it as a cautionary tale, her fatal driving error having almost certainly been caused by the presence in her bloodstream of both anti-depressant medication and alcohol.

The Belgian chocolates, discovered some weeks later, when Jennifer's desk drawer was cleared, were, because it seemed a shame to waste them, passed round the office by the same junior who had informed her of Noel's disappearance. Noel himself selected one that was garnished with crystallised violet petals.

Until he took early retirement at the age of forty-nine, Noel Sloane continued to meet the modest demands his work imposed upon him, and to be the dour, dull, moody man his colleagues and indeed his quietly nervous wife had always considered him to be. When he thought of Jennifer, which he occasionally did, it was with a vague sense of regret, not because she was dead but that she had failed to love him.

Because it had always been beyond his imagination to enter the mind of his beloved, he had no notion of the consequences of his feelings for her. Which, for him, was just as well.

# Western Approaches

"Western Approaches" is part of an on-going project involving a collection of shorter pieces that are linked by World War Two.

A scatter of people had already gathered, grouped like standing stones, dark, against the shiny sand, watching the blurred shapes of the two small craft, lifting on the swell, solidifying slowly, each wave moving them closer to the shore. As though the sea wanted to be rid of them. To abandon them among the debris from previous tides.

The lifeboat rode behind the crabber, which had taken it in tow. As the wave lifted first one, then the other, the two boats tilted and slid down its smooth face, the line between them slackening. Then, as they came off the wave and the crabber once more took the weight of the tow, the rope snapped taut, flinging an arc of spray into the still air.

Arch Trethewey, at the helm of his crab boat, squinted back through the half-light at the three figures, wedged, one against the other, a single, rigid outline in the lifeboat's bow, as though braced to resist its movement. Arch swung his tiller, searching instinctively for the dying breeze, trying to keep his sail filled. The occasional flog of his canvas was the only sound that night as the watchers stood and waited.

Sometimes explosions rocked the sea beyond their horizon and objects were found, sprawled at low tide on the flat, wet sand. Ropes, lifejackets, cartons of food—sodden and salty—salvage from merchantmen torpedoed in the Western Approaches. Once there had been oranges, scattered like beads from a broken necklace along the high-water line, and gathered greedily by the village kids. There were lifebelts. Boots. And bodies. Oiled like stricken seabirds. Burned, some of them. Picked at by gulls. Crab-eaten.

As the lifeboat's keel nudged the sand the soft impact was enough to dislodge its cargo. Two of the figures swayed, rigid, but the third toppled forward, sprawling loosely across the oily floorboards.

On the beach, Molly, watching, moved her lips, unconsciously mouthing words she had learned in school that day. "Then saw they how there hove a dusky barge... . Dark as a funeral scarf from stem to stern... . And all her decks were dense with stately forms..."

The survivor was lifted from the boat and laid on an oilskin, spread across the hard sand. Four men took its weight and began the journey up the beach to the village.

The air was thickening into darkness now, but as they carried him past her, Molly saw the silver skin, smudged with oil, and the half-closed eyes. Something about "a wind on a wasteland..." Boots were crushing the shingle at the top of the beach.

At the water's edge people gathered to peer into the lifeboat. As Molly stepped forward to join them Rose Penarth put a gnarled hand on her shoulder. "No," she said. And she turned the child and walked behind her up towards the lights of the village—for despite the blackout there was light there. Small, yellowish pools of it, lying guiltily in front of open doors. Sharp slivers, escaping the edges of hastily drawn curtains.

That night torchlight slashed the darkness. Molly left her bed and from her window saw the truck, the red cross just visible on its side.

Headlights shrouded, engine idling, noisy in the darkness, it took on its cargo. On one stretcher the injured man lay wrapped in scarlet blankets, his head supported by a pillow. But the second and third stretchers were shrouded, the inert figures concealed. The dead and the half-dead. "And from them rose a cry…" The truck lurched off, labouring uphill, its dimmed lights washing across the faces of the blind-eyed cottages. The couple of villagers who had opened their doors to stand and watch, turned away and closed them now.

Molly's feet felt as cold as the bare floorboards under them. Her teeth chattered and she shuddered in her thin nightdress, standing, half-asleep, transfixed by the events of that night, looking down at the empty street. But the street was not empty.

They must have come from the beach. She had not seen them come but now they stood, the two of them, motionless, there, or not there, she was uncertain, facing the point where the truck had vanished from their view and they had looked, in the first greyness of the dawn, like the two men Molly had seen lifted, rigid, from the lifeboat. Bodies, they had been. With their faces decently covered. She had seen them loaded onto a handcart and hauled up the beach. So they couldn't be there, standing in the dawn, in the empty street. And then they weren't there. Where she had thought they had been there was only empty shadow now. Molly closed her eyes and turned away from the window, choosing not to see them. Not to look back, in case they were there again.

She shuddered down into her bed, absorbing its warmth. The worn sheet felt soft. The rough blanket and lumpy coverlet, reassuring. But her mind seethed with sounds and shapes. There was something in the poem about stars. How did it go?

As she lay, thoughts and limbs slowly dissolving together as the warmth of her bed soothed her, the half-remembered words tangled into the images she'd seen that evening, sliding over and under, like cloud layers on wild, moony nights, until the lines of the poem had unravelled.

She slept, haunted, as she would always be, by the scene on the half-forgotten beach, by the three dark figures in the drifting boat, by the dead and the half-dead. "Black-stoled, black-hooded, like a dream." And she sensed, as she would often sense, the silent cry that had risen "and echoed to the tingling stars."

# Flirting With Vincent

"Flirting With Vincent" was originally transmitted in the form of a thirty-minute radio play, which was broadcast on Radio Four in 1995.

.

Her heart was beating a little faster than usual that morning as she proceeded with the almost ceremonial preparation of her breakfast. She sliced an orange into halves, took one in her palm, inverted it and pressed it firmly down onto the Citromatic—a neat appliance, given to her on her retirement by a colleague. A more formal gift, a cheque for a substantial sum, had paid for the electric shower unit in Miss Thompson's new bathroom.

Juice collected in the section of the device, which was designed for that purpose, and from which Miss Thompson decanted it into the particular cut-glass tumbler that always featured on her breakfast tray. Setting this beside the one slice of unbuttered, wholemeal toast and the bowl of muesli moistened with semi-skimmed milk, she lifted the tray and carried it out into the small, south-facing conservatory, which, she noticed, still smelled faintly of drying cement and, less acceptably, of the local workman who had only recently completed its construction.

It was here that her already raised heartbeat quickened, triggering that tiresome feeling of anxiety that, Miss Thompson knew, would be followed by what she refused to call, even to herself, a "flush". A condition that, her doctor had advised her fifteen years previously, would, in the fullness of time, pass, but which, irritatingly, had not. And here she was, slightly more than sixty years old, the sweatings and flushings still mocking an expired and always under-used sexuality. She mopped her brow, sipped orange juice and attempted to divert her mind.

Her painting materials lay ready for today's work. The palette, purchased while she had lived in London, from a supplier of artists' materials, just off the King's Road, had been anointed, thoroughly, on the previous evening, with linseed oil. Tubes of primary colours were set out promisingly, in a neat row, together with pristine brushes and several thin charcoal sticks. A rectangular canvas, stretched, primed and virginal, stood against the wall.

Miss Thompson's energy level climbed as she spooned up the muesli, glancing, as she did so, at an illustrated book on the life of Vincent van Gogh, which lay open at a particular page, beside her on the breakfast table.

The cause of this morning's excitement was that yesterday, on her walk and always on the look-out for suitable subjects to paint, Miss Thompson had seen a mass of rooks whirling into the sky above a field of green barley. She had been reminded, vividly, though unsurprisingly, of van Gogh's final canvases, where blues and golds rise, incandescent and demented, into rook-strewn skies. Miss Thompson had experienced a familiar stirring of compassion for the lonely figure, which her mind's eye at once conjured and placed in her barley field. She was moved, not for the first time, by the story of the man's desperation, his despair, his self-destruction. And she determined, then, to make her own painting of this similar scene and to try to define in it the truth of her own feelings and sensibilities. The secrets, passions and desperations of her own long, solitary and uneventful life.

She felt light-headed and nervous—almost as though she was going to confession. Not that she ever had been to confession, but she was aware that she was preparing to expose her soul, to reveal herself as she had never done before, even to herself. It would only be to herself, of course. No one else need ever see the resulting picture. She could, and almost certainly would, shortly after its completion, paint over it, obliterating it with white primer. It would be gone forever. As though it had never existed. But for a while, for as long as she wanted it, could tolerate it, it would exist. And it would be, must be, an absolutely true statement about herself.

She had by now become so agitated that she was barely able to finish eating her toast. It was then, just as she decided to turn her back on the washing-up and go immediately out, into the field, set up her easel and begin work on the painting, that she heard the cattle.

There was nothing unusual in this. Miss Thompson's retreat, which had once been a labourer's cottage set on a wedge-shaped quarter-acre of land, distinguished by three mature pine trees, had belonged to a nearby farm and was bounded on one side by a lane and on the other by the twenty-acre field, now thick with the waving green barley that had caught her attention on the previous day. So the sound of cattle was perfectly normal. What was not normal, this morning, was that the herd, having broken through from the pasture in which it had been grazing, had invaded the barley field. Miss Thompson knew why. The drinking trough in the pasture that abutted the foot of her garden and in which the cattle had originally been confined, was cracked and empty. The previous days having been unusually hot, Miss Thompson had heard the thirsting creatures sucking on the mud in the base of the trough, and now, desperate for water, they had broken through, into the barley field, in their quest for it.

Arnold West, whose farm it was, had, twelve months previously, sold the cottage to Miss Thompson in an attempt to reduce an overdraft that neither he, nor his bank manager, could any longer support. Childless and recently widowed, Arnold had tried, since this welcome injection of Miss Thompson's cash, to consolidate his financial position, limit his overheads and survive. But, day by day, he was failing, struggling, single-handed, with leaking barns, sick stock, marauding foxes, broken-down equipment, and with his own impaired health and increasing depression. Stacks of paperwork had, since the onset of his wife's last illness and subsequent death, accumulated relentlessly in his dank office. For it was she, of the two of them, who had possessed the greater aptitude for figures and for the endless form-filling that, if properly exploited, yielded the grants, subsidies and allowances on which the economics of present-day farming are based.

Miss Thompson knew Arnold West's telephone number, and on several occasions over the preceding months had used it. Once it was because she had observed a dog, worrying his ewes. On another occasion she had been the first to report to him the invasion of one of his pastures by a group of New Age travellers, who had set up a camp that the local council had taken six months to remove. She dialled his number now, visualising, as she waited for him to answer the exterior bell, his stooping, booted figure, making its way across the yard, skirting piles of reeking dung.

"Yes," came his voice at last, its tone defensive, as though whatever the news was, it would be bad and he would be expecting it.

"I'm so sorry to bother you, Mr West," said Miss Thompson, "but your cows—steers, I suppose I mean—have broken into the barley field next door to me…" She paused. Was he still there? Had he heard her? "Mr West?"

He thanked her. He sounded weary. Resigned. He rang off.

Miss Thompson climbed the narrow stairs to her bedroom. From its tiny, gingham-curtained window she could see the steers plunging about in the barley, trampling it dreadfully. It occurred to her that it was going to be difficult for Arnold West, single-handed, to round up the excited beasts and drive them back, through the gaping hole they had created in the hedge, into the dry pasture from which they had fled. If only he had repaired the trough in the first place, none of this would have happened and she would be, by now, at her easel, laying in the shapes and lines of her painting. But he had neglected the trough as he neglected so many of the endless tasks that confronted him each day, working, she knew, as long as his strength allowed him, like a man baling a leaking boat, struggling against a rising water-level. Obviously, she should turn out to help him. Pull on her green rubber boots, zip up her stiff, new, Barbour jacket, and, armed with a stout stick, put herself at his disposal. But her dread of cattle prevented her. She had brought with her from Lewisham an unshakeable fear of their blundering strength. However much she tried to persuade herself that by shouting and waving a stick the creatures would give way to her, she quailed at the thought of putting theory into practice. Consequently the routes of her forays into the countryside and the subjects of her painting expeditions were dictated by the presence or the absence in the surrounding fields, of Arnold West's livestock. Of his sheep she had little fear, though there had been one occasion when, surrounded by forty-five pairs of inquisitive eyes, she had felt seriously intimidated.

She heard the tractor come up the lane and pass her

cottage. From her bedroom window she watched Arnold West enter the field on foot and trudge towards his defiant herd. She saw the beasts lunging and plunging around him. Saw the man wading about in the wrecked crop, waving his stick. Heard him shouting as he tracked back and forth across the field, the cattle cavorting, separating and then forming tight, jostling groups, slipping past his outstretched arms, plundering and flattening the barley.

Dorothy Thompson turned, guiltily, from the sight, plugged in her vacuum cleaner and spent the next half-hour noisily and unnecessarily Hoovering her cottage from top to bottom. Eventually, switching off the machine, she listened for sounds from the field.... There was silence. She waited, her guilty conscience easing. Self-justification rescuing her from shame. He could hardly expect her, a retired lady of uncertain health, to assist him. It simply wasn't her problem. If the farm was too much for him, he should either give it up or hire some labour. Had his herd been properly watered it would not have broken out of the field and her day would not have been disrupted. It was, however, still only just after ten o'clock. She need not, after all, abandon her plan.

Easel under one arm, folding stool under the other, her bag of materials slung over her shoulder, Miss Thompson walked the short distance from her cottage to the gate of the barley field and went through it.

She had already decided precisely where she would position her easel. A track through the barley had, she felt, led the eye nicely to a stone barn that stood, picturesquely crumbling, on the far side of the field, the gaps in its lichen-covered slates exposing weather-bleached rafters and purlins. But today the track had almost vanished in the general destruction wrought by the cattle. Sunlight glittered on the broken shafts of barley stalks and on the crushed, drooping, bearded heads. The ground at her feet was churned by hooves. She stepped gingerly through a spattering of fresh dung. But the rooks, wheeling and flapping, making ugly, jagged black shapes against the sky, were as evocative as they had been on the previous day. At the sight of them and in the context of today's events, Miss Thompson felt a stirring in her soul. This was what she wanted. This was what she intended her picture to be about. Desperation. Destruction. Passion. What she…Dorothy Thompson…Miss…Civil Servant (retired)…recognised, understood, shared, yes, shared…with Vincent van Gogh. She could do it. Would do it. Today. Now.

Rapidly, fingers shaking, she set out her materials, laying the tubes of oils in a row on the palette, clamping the canvas to the easel and, taking a charcoal stick delicately between finger and thumb, fastened her eyes and her mind upon her subject. But, as she raised her hand, tremulously to the white rectangle of canvas, she became aware of a figure moving through the gateway.

Arnold West, for some reason, had returned. He did not see her and went slowly forward, into the crushed barley and towards the centre of the field.

Miss Thompson, blinking into the strong light, watched. At first she intended to attract his attention to her presence, to commiserate with him over the damaged crop. Even, perhaps, to apologise and offer excuses for the fact that she had felt unable to help him drive out his herd. But he was moving away from her. And in his hands he carried something. A stick? She squinted into the sunlight. No. Not a stick. A gun. A shotgun.

The sun was very bright. The man stopped and stood

alone and motionless. A stooped, dark figure, silhouetted against the shining, ravaged crop. Leaning, wretched and weary, on his gun. Miss Thompson, watching, felt her mouth go dry and her heart lurch unpleasantly in her narrow chest as the scene before her blurred alarmingly into another. One with which she was all too familiar. One which was reproduced in full colour on the glossy page of a book that at this moment lay open in her conservatory, beside her abandoned breakfast tray...

"It's the rooks," she breathed, inhaling deeply, in an attempt to calm herself. "He's going to shoot the rooks!" But it was another thought, one which she could not utter, but which she knew was the truth, that filled her mind and stopped her breath, immobilising her when she should have run forward, waved her arms, distracted him. Silencing her when she should have called to him, shouted to him, "Don't do it! Don't! Please, Mr West! Wait!"

Sunlight struck the barrels of the gun, briefly dazzling her as he turned it and leaned forward over it. She saw him reaching down. As though in slow motion, she speechlessly... uselessly...watched as he slid his hand down the length of the barrel, stretching his fingers, groping for the trigger.

The police were kind. A young, female constable made her a cup of strong tea before they took her statement. But she became distressed as she related the morning's events to them, tears running down her face and her throat tightening until she could only gulp "I should have...I didn't...I ought to have..."

"Don't upset yourself," they said. "There was nothing you could have done." And they were probably right. She did so want them to be right.

After they left she remembered her painting things,

scattered in the field where she had left them when she ran to telephone for help. She had better fetch them. But why? Her flirtation with oil painting was, she knew, over. The cottage, alone in the rolling landscape, suddenly no longer seemed the setting for the great adventure of her retirement. She felt exposed here. Vulnerable. A stranger in an alien world. But what should she do? She could hardly return to Lewisham and have all her Ministry friends laughing behind their hands and saying, "We told her so."

Miss Thompson sat in her sitting room for a considerable time. The day clouded over, the wind rose and heavy rain began to fall. The cup of tea the policewoman had made for her had grown cool and then cold in her hands.

Eventually she rose and went out into the conservatory. Rain was drumming on the glazed roof and gurgling in the new down-pipe. The garden was a mass of dripping greenery. The book of van Gogh's collected works still lay open on the table. Without looking at the painting of the rooks she closed the book, lifted her breakfast tray and carried it into the kitchen.

Detergent foamed reliably in the hot water and her hands slipped into her pink rubber gloves in a reassuring way. She would not, she decided as she stacked the dishes onto the drainer, allow these farming people to spoil things for her. Nor would she spend any more time on morbid, suicidal painters. She would use flowers as her subjects. Yes, she would. Wild flowers from the hedgerows. She would paint lots of little watercolours and post them to friends. To her less fortunate, city-bound friends. That's what she would do.

Then something caught her eye. Something flashing past the double-glazed pane of her kitchen window. Something dark, wild and sudden. Then another. And another. Things jagged and black, that dived and swooped. Her eye was drawn up towards the highest branches of her pine trees where the sky above her garden was being darkened by rooks. They wheeled clumsily, clustering into tight groups, then banking, fanning out, skidding, fast, down the wind, zigzagging dangerously between the limbs of the trees. They hurtled towards her. Threateningly. Challengingly. Accusing her. Finding her wanting. She gripped the slippery edge of her sink with her rubber-gloved fingers and shut her eyes. But there he was. Vincent. In her head. With his bandaged ear, his cornfield. And his rooks, like pieces of charred paper, beating round him, fragmented, tormenting. She banished him by opening her eyes, turning her head away from the window and groping for the blind-pull. She must exclude the rooks, shield her eyes from that awful image, from the connection it made with the worse image, the image of the man, the desperate man, alone in a field with a gun. But her fingers blundered and the small pine knob on the end of the cord bounced away from her. She reached for it, grabbed at it as it went past her but missed again, reached further and lost her balance. The small mat, on which she stood at her sink, skidded from under her and she was falling. She shut her eyes, flinching from the inevitable impact as she struck the floor. In that split second another figure invaded the dark space behind her closed lids. Not Vincent. This figure was moving through green barley. Then stopping. Reaching down…Miss Thompson was stumbling over the uneven ground, the tangle of trampled stalks slowing and tripping her. She was shouting.

"No! Don't do it! Wait!" She reached the man and flung herself forward, gripping the barrel of the gun in both her hands. Then her world exploded. The back of her head had struck the terracotta tiles of her kitchen floor with a force that cracked her skull.

The coroner described it as a freak accident possibly caused in part by the trauma experienced by the deceased as a result of her witnessing, at close hand, another tragic event, earlier on the same day.

# I, Said The Sparrow

"I, Said The Sparrow" is another story with its origins in World War Two. Its transmission date is to be announced.

Connie hadn't brushed her hair or changed out of the old jogging pants and sweater she had pulled on when she got out of her bed that morning. It didn't much matter how she looked. It never had. She put the key into the lock of the main door at the end of the Nissen hut.

It was more than sixty years since the Yanks had erected the hut. They had used it as an officers' mess during their preparations for the D-Day landings. That had been the year before Connie's birth. Since then it had served as the village hall. Wedding receptions were held there. Bingo. And the hops that they called discos nowadays. It was Connie's job, as it had been her mother's before her, to tidy up after these occasions, to clean the toilets, put the tables and chairs in order and sweep the floor.

As a toddler, seated squarely on the window seat, Connie had watched her mother go through this ritual with the same resigned expression on her face as she, she guessed, was herself wearing, this grey, November afternoon. Sometimes, when money had been particularly short, her mother had picked through the leftovers, the half-eaten sausage rolls and jam tarts, and found, even in those food-rationed days, enough for their supper.

Last night the Fishing Club—having recently re-invented itself as the Anglers' Association—had held its annual party. Now, as Connie entered the hut she walked into cold, stale air, which reeked of alcohol and tobacco smoke. The empties, being the hirers' responsibility, were gone. And the glasses.

Cans, cardboard plates and food wrappers along with the contents of the ashtrays, had been dumped into black plastic bags, which now stood, knotted, by the door.

It was quiet. Just the swish of Connie's broom across the lino. Earlier, the baying of hounds, carried, with a spatter of rain, on a rising westerly wind, had told her that the hunt was on the high ground above Blackstone House. Connie knew the house well. She spent three hours a week cleaning it for the Stratton family who owned it. Their estate manager, a florid, hard-pressed man, was also master of the foxhounds, which Connie could hear, closer now, probably working through the woods that bordered the river.

Each Thursday at noon, when Connie had completed her work at the house, Mrs Stratton handed over the two five-pound notes that were her wages and gave her a cup of coffee and three ginger biscuits. Connie did not care for ginger, and she would have preferred tea.

Mrs Stratton had a curious habit of sitting at the kitchen table and watching Connie while she drank the coffee and chewed the biscuits. She would light a cigarette, occasionally offering one to Connie, who always declined, her unimportance confirmed, once again, by the fact that Mrs Stratton never remembered whether she did or did not smoke.

Connie felt obliged, out of politeness, to attempt conversation with this woman who sat, her expressionless eyes focussed on Connie's, but barely seeing her and rarely responding to her. Mrs Stratton made Connie feel that everything she said was foolish. That her opinions were irrelevant. That for her to expect her employer to pay attention to her views, on this subject or that, amounted almost to impertinence. Connie was used to this sensation. No one had ever valued what she thought or paid any attention to her when she spoke her mind. She had learned to keep her feelings to herself.

Her weekly visit to Blackstone House and Mrs Stratton's cold stare had become a low point in her monotonous week. Sundays, sweep the church ready for morning service. Mondays, clean the lavatories at the primary school. Tuesdays, go with the Meals On Wheels lady, delivering the dinners. Wednesdays, an hour as "home help" for a confused old widow woman who never recognised Connie, and wondered why she had come knocking on her door.

"It's Connie, Mrs Tring. Come to clean."

Thursdays, Mrs Stratton. Fridays, minding Mrs Stratton's twin grandchildren, while her daughter Edwina met friends for coffee. And on Saturday afternoons Connie put the village hall to rights after whatever function had reduced it to chaos on the previous evening, and prepared it for what was to take place there that night.

She picked up two of the plastic bags and hauled them out to the bins. The wind pulled at her. Over the years, the Nissen hut had, from time to time, been repaired. Its windows, chimney flue and the wide doors at each end had all been replaced. But the original shell, the carapace, had survived untouched and was now so thickly crusted with mosses and lichens that it blended into the hillside, seeming almost to be part of the rising ground and the sweeping, leafless, winter landscape.

There was a snapshot, faded now to a brownish grey, that had been taken during the war. It showed the Nissen hut, newly erected. In the doorway, their arms linked, were Connie's mother and an American soldier, smart in his uniform. When she was dying Connie's mother had, for the first time, shown the picture to her daughter.

87

"Keep it safe, Con," she had whispered. "'Tis your dad, see." Her eyes were focussed on the past and she seemed barely aware of the effect of her words. "There was dances..." she said, almost inaudibly. "Local girls and the GIs from the camp over Longcombe. That's where I met 'im. The two of us would sneak back to the hut, after."

Her mother's grey face was soft with reminiscence. Connie sat holding the bony hand, her mind resisting the confusing thoughts her mother was putting into it. Wasn't it enough that the hand Connie held felt fragile and unfamiliar? Not plump and warm and rough, as it had always been? That her mother was sick and going to die?

After that, Connie often paused in her cleaning work to let her glance wander round the bleak interior of the hut. Where did they do it, she wondered. Her mother and the man who was her father. On the floor? Behind the stacked tables? Or on that wide bench below the window? Somewhere in this inhospitable, silent space, her life had been started. But it was another man altogether who had raised her and given her his name. A local lad with a weak chest that had made him unfit for military service, had been there, when no one else was, to marry Connie's mother when she needed it. And to act like he was Connie's dad all those years. And then die without a word about it three days before her twelfth birthday. No one, until long after his death, had thought to tell Connie what he'd done for her. She wished she had known. He had been good to her. She would have thanked him.

The man in the snapshot had been killed on Omaha Beach. Or so her mother said. But how could you tell what was true? He'd be old now, if he'd lived. And somewhere in America. With a grown family. Grandchildren even. And never knowing he had a daughter in England called Connie. Who did cleaning.

She stood near the open doorway, her broom in her hands, thinking about her dead mother and her two dead fathers. The light was fading. Behind her the interior of the hut was a dark void. The hunt was closer now. The noise of the hounds giving tongue made Connie's skin crawl. She stood, the gale roaring in the tops of the trees, and stared down the length of the overhung pathway. She could sense the impact of hooves on hard earth. The shouts of the unseen riders tangled with the baying of the pack as the confused mass approached, bunching, as horsemen and dogs converged in the narrow valley.

Then she saw the fox and felt the hairs rise on the nape of her neck. He was running close to the ground, ears flat, eyes huge, tongue lolling. Connie heard the master encouraging the pack to spread, to chase, to corner and kill its quarry.

The fox streaked towards the open doorway, through it and on, into the darkness beyond it. As he passed Connie his eyes flicked briefly in her direction. The brown, desperate look took away her breath but she had reached for the door, slammed it shut behind him and was standing with her back to it, leaning on her broom, when the first of the hounds spilled out of the undergrowth. They spread, muzzles down, casting for the scent of the fox, following it to her feet.

Connie stood her ground as the dogs bounded round her, but her eyes were on the rider, the master, clamped like a clothes peg to his huge mare, his face purplish under the black peak of his velvet hat, the buttons on his pink coat straining. Looming over her he reined in, the mare fighting the bit, both man and mount breathing noisily. Connie smiled up at him.

"I seen your ol' fox!" she said, before he could ask. "Come right up to me, 'e did! Then 'e ran back!" The mare was fidgeting and blowing, its flanks lathered, its eyes as bloodshot as its rider's.

"Back, you say?" He was breathless. Almost beyond speech. Connie looked up at the flushed face. One day a vein would burst and he would pitch from his saddle, fall like an oak and never move again. She nodded to where the hounds were circling. Would he believe her? There was no point in her saying the fox had run past her into the trees because its scent ended at the hut door. There were only two possibilities. Either the animal had taken refuge inside the building, or it had doubled back, down the path.

"Yeah!" she said. "Back the way 'e come, the varmint!" She brandished her broom. "I'd have had 'e for sure if 'e'd come close enough!" Then the man was pulling the mare's head round. He was jabbing his heels into her sides. He was lurching off down the path. He was calling the hounds to order. He was gone.

Connie waited until the clamour of the hunt was lost in the sound of the gale. Then she opened the door, and leaving it wide behind her walked the length of the hut, pushed open the second door and propped it with her broom.

She moved aside and stood quite still, her heart beating heavily while she peered into the corners of the hut, into the shadows under the stacked chairs and tables. There was no sign of the fox. Perhaps he had already fled to safety without her seeing him go. Then she spotted the eyes. Wide. Shining. Dark as pitch. Locked onto hers. He was crouched under the window bench, the seat on which her mother had lain down, all those years ago, with the man in the snapshot. Connie was certain it was there that it had happened. Under that window. It would have been a soft night, leaves filtering the moonlight. A nightingale perhaps. There had been nightingales, then. It would have been a moment of significance. Connie felt the warmth of this significance coursing through her and relished the sensation. She was Connie. Connie somebody. Because of her, there in the shadows, her fox was safely breathing. Moments passed. Then, the tip of his brush pale as a primrose, he crossed the space between his hiding place and the open door. Connie glimpsed him as he went, a rusty blur moving against undergrowth, which, as he darted suddenly sideways, instantly and absolutely absorbed him.

She switched on the lights, blinked in their brilliance and finished the cleaning. The hut was in order now and smelling pleasantly of the lavender-scented polish she had sprayed onto the wood of the window seat. She turned off the lights, locked the doors and dropped the keys into her pocket.

As she made her way down the path, her eyes adjusting to the half-light, she was smiling. Somewhere out there something was alive, which, but for her, would have been dead. She, Connie. Connie anybody, it didn't seem to matter now—had had her way. She had altered something. Her will had prevailed.

The next time she was offered ginger biscuits she would politely decline. "And I'd rather have tea, Mrs Stratton, if it's all the same to you."

# Solitaire

"Solitaire" was produced by Viv Beeby, BBC Bristol and transmitted in December 1996. The reader was Philip Franks.

Had he believed she would do it, he would have physically prevented her. It would not have been difficult. Instead, he sat slumped at the table, a wine bottle in one hand, a cigarette burning between the fingers of the other, watching her as she plunged about, gathering her few belongings.

She wasn't looking at him now. The hours of accusation and anger were over. Her eyes were dry, though she breathed unevenly, throat and chest tight, as she moved, fast, between the two rooms, bare feet whispering across the lino.

Drawing the nicotine into him, narrowing his eyes against the smoke, his eyes followed her. The sound, as he exhaled, was a sigh of exasperation. From time to time he raised the bottle and drank.

He thought she wouldn't go. He thought she hadn't the courage. The journey out would be daunting. Too daunting, for her. Not merely a short drive across town to some sympathetic woman-friend or to her mother's welcoming house. There was no woman-friend. No mother. No town, even.

Soon it would be dark. The highway was four hours away along a track that was rough and hard to follow. The van was unreliable. In the morning when the sun rose, early and blinding, the heat would become so extreme that, if stranded, she and the kids would not make it through the day. She knew that. So she wouldn't go.

His eyes, watching her, were hard. Like a lizard's eyes. Or a snake's. She wondered how it was that she hadn't seen the hardness. She had thought him brilliant. Excusing his behaviour as the eccentricity of an artist, the unrecognised genius whom she would nurture. He had seemed vulnerable. Focussed. But slowly he had revealed himself. Blow by blow she'd felt the shock of him. The wilful irresponsibility. The brutality of his selfishness. The callousness. Now she understood. Perceiving him at last, through the veils that had shrouded her from the truth of him.

It was four years since they had left the city to live in opal country near Yowah. Since then, while he had painted the strange terrain and its bizarre inhabitants, pouring wine down his throat and kippering his damaged lungs, his stark, wild canvases accumulating, she had given birth to twin boys. Conceived, carried and delivered them in the sweltering hut, with its creaking iron roof, its verandah throwing a dense shadow on the surrounding sun-bleached grit.

While she suckled her babies and weaned them, her only friend had been the old man. The old, lunatic man. The old, mad fossicking man. Charlie. With his crazy stories of his cache of opals.

They had sat together, she and Charlie. Countless hours in the thick shade of the verandah, dazed by the heat, taking it in turns to play solitaire. Charlie would arrive with the Hessian bag swinging on its drawstring, the marbles rattling against the worn, wooden board, his threadbare pocket bulging round a whisky bottle. Reaching into the bag, the woman would withdraw the marbles, a handful at a time, and as Charlie watched, placing the bottle carefully against his chair-leg, would set one into each shallow indentation of the board, her foot rocking the cradle in which her boys lay, fretful and clammy in the heat.

The marbles caught and reflected the brilliance of the

glaring sun. Like the pale eyes of the woman, the lonely woman, the damaged woman, who was withering before old Charlie's eyes.

Finishing her game, she'd shrug and smile, pushing the board towards him.

"Your go, Charlie," she would say, her voice barely more than a sigh.

And he'd tell her, as he moved the marbles on the board, of his years of fossicking, of his finds and his disappointments. Of the folk he'd seen come and go. Good men and bad, kind and cruel, the idle and the obsessed. A few had made it back into the world, rich beyond their dreams. Most, broken, their strength and resolution sweated out of them, had wandered off. Some into their graves among the diggings. But Charlie had stayed on, longer than any, his cache of stones slowly accumulating.

He'd describe them to her, how the colours flashed and flickered, concealing and revealing the fires that had created them, telling her how to distinguish valuable gems from worthless opaline. And when she asked him why he'd never left, never taken his stones to the city, sold them and spent the money they would fetch, he'd shake his head and smile, squinting out into the glare.

"Reckon this'll do me," he would say. And she wondered, watching as his calloused fingers moved the marbles on the solitaire board, whether it was true, what people said, that he had few gems of any worth, that his fabulous collection existed only in a mind addled by the hot sun, clouded by the whisky with which he deadened the aches in his old, bruised bones.

"You shouldn't be here, girl," he'd say to her, when she was pale and tired, breast-feeding the sickly babies too long because it was cheaper than making the journey to the town for formula milk. "It's no place for you." And his eyes would slide past her to rest accusingly on the young man...

She dumped the duffle bags into the truck, loaded spare cans of petrol and of water, spread sleeping bags in the back for her kids. And still the man sat motionless at the table. One by one she lifted the drowsing children from their beds and settled them in the truck. Finally she returned to the kitchen and met the man's eyes.

He was rolling his next cigarette, his un-watched fingers performing the familiar sequence of movements, heavy lidded eyes fixed on the woman's face.

"I'm going now," was all she said. His features twisted slightly, into something approaching a smile. A battered tin of cannabis resin clattered to the floor as his chair scraped back and he lurched to his feet, weaving slightly in the cramped, dark space, expecting another long, wrangling row. But the woman turned abruptly and went out into the darkness. The keys were already in the ignition switch and the engine fired at once, noisily, in the silence. Dust flew as the tyres spun and then gripped.

The horizon ahead of her was piled with bruised cloud that dwarfed the mulga-studded scrubland. The children wedged themselves against pillows, stuck their thumbs into their mouths, watched their mother's face in the driving mirror and felt the truck slam into second gear.

By the time the man stumbled out onto the verandah the truck's taillights were already blurred, smudged by the rising dust. As the reality of her departure reached him and he hurled her name uselessly after her, a sensation, which neither wine nor drugs would deaden, began to hollow out his chest.

The track climbed slightly from the shallow valley. As it levelled off, the woman felt the engine ease. In the driving-mirror the darkness closed behind her. He might try to follow. The single beam from the headlight of his old trials bike was what she feared to see, closing the distance between them. But nothing was visible beyond the eerie, red glow of her own taillights while her headlights dazzled on the pale sand of the track, accentuating the movement of the vehicle as it plunged over the potholed surface. She eased her back against the seat and flexed her fingers, changing her grip on the wheel, bracing herself for the long hours of driving that lay ahead. Then, caught weirdly by her lights, a vague blur solidified directly in her path. She braked hard and the wheels locked into a dusty slither. The children, thrown forward, protested, struggled with their sleeping bags and peered, as the woman was peering, through the windscreen.

It was the old man. He shuffled towards them, head down, smiling, and came round to the side window.

"I could have killed you, Charlie!"

He leaned in, the hooded eyes scanning her face. He was inches from her and she could smell the reek of sweat, tobacco and stale booze. She could see the leathery pores of his grimed skin. His eyes narrowed as he read her face.

"You'm goin', ain't cha," he said, resigned to her departure. "And not before time. I shall miss yer. Here." He was holding something out to her. Pushing it in through the truck window.

"Take it, girlie." The marbles rattled. The Hessian bag was rough against her resisting hand.

"No, Charlie! I couldn't!"

"Go on!" he insisted. "Have it as a keepsake!" He stepped

back, turned, and was instantly absorbed by the indigo darkness.

She called out to him. What would he do without his lonely game? Especially now she was gone!

"Charlie!" But there was no answer, no sound beyond the idling of the truck engine.

It was after midnight when she drove through the town and out onto the highway. Two hours later she pulled into a wayside motel.

The dreary room was dank. Its overworked air conditioner rattled and dripped. She laid the sleeping babies in one of the two beds and stood a long time, letting the lukewarm water of the shower flow over her.

Past sleep, she lay exhausted in the darkness, shaken by the heavy thump of her heartbeat. Shivering, unused to the chilled air, she pulled the covers over herself but still could not sleep.

A conversation was taking place in her head. Two parts of her mind, speaking at once, the thoughts colliding. "How has this happened? Why have I done this? Why now? Because he did not love us. Not me. Not the boys." She began to calm. To feel more resolute. Stronger. Harder. The first part of her mind fell silent. "Because he doesn't care for us, provide for us or protect us. Because we would have died of him, if we'd stayed in that place, the kids sickening, while he drank the money."

She reached across the empty space beside her in the bed, moving her hand over the tightly stretched, chill sheet, the hard, smooth pillow. It was over. She was out. Away. Alone. The regular breathing of her children seemed to isolate her further. She withdrew her hand and finally, exhausted, slipped into a shallow sleep from which, subconsciously overtaken by panic, she soon woke, abruptly overwhelmed by the realisation that she had planned nothing beyond her departure. Where should she go? How could she survive? She switched on the light. Two hours yet, of darkness. She must be calm. She must rest. Sleep was clearly impossible. But she must not think, because in these small, unnerving hours of darkness, thought might drive her back to the man and to the life from which she and her children must escape. She reached for the remote-control switch but the noise of the television would wake the children. There were no books in the room. Not even a Gideon Bible in the bedside drawer. But the solitaire board, in its Hessian bag, was in her duffle bag. She loosened the drawstring, and tipped the contents out onto the bedcover.

There was more than the board and the marbles in the bag. At first she thought the gleaming chunks were simply opaline. But as she examined them, turning them slowly in the light, and saw the glint of rich, outrageous colour, she perceived their value. These were not the cheap trophies of an amateur fossicker. This was the pick of Charlie's finds, the result of all his years of labour in the opal diggings.

Of course she could not accept them. She cursed him, knowing she must return the opals to him. Knowing that to leave Yowah a second time might prove impossible for her. "Damn you, Charlie!" She unfolded a twist of paper that lay among the stones. Words had been laboriously printed with a blunt pencil. She tilted them towards the light.

"I don't want no nonsense, girlie," she read. "Them's more use to you than to me and anyhow there's plenty more where they come from. Take 'em to the address on the card. He's an honest bloke and'll give a fair price for 'em. Good luck from your friend...Charlie." A dog-eared business card bore the name and address of a gemstone dealer in the city.

In the black night at Yowah a sudden silence woke the young man. The Tilley lamp, having sucked the last of its supply of kerosene, had abruptly ceased its hissing. Groggily, he raised his throbbing head... "Darl...?" he said, getting to his feet. He reeled towards the silent fridge in which the contents were already barely chilled and groped for a can of beer. He stumbled out onto the verandah and dropped into a creaking wicker chair whose cushions smelled faintly of the children who had played in it that day.

Cursing as the warm beer foamed out, he lay back in the chair and fixed his eyes on an almost indistinguishable point where the dense land met the paler sky. The point where, should the woman return, he would first see her headlights probing the darkness. But he knew now that she would not return. Had she lost her resolve it would have been sooner than this. Before the accumulating hours and miles of the separation had worked on her. "Darl...?" he whispered, querulously. The silence snuffed the word. Now he was alone, cowering beneath the moonless arc of the sky and the senselessly spinning stars.

The woman reread Charlie's note several times and stared for a while at the objects scattered on the bedcover. Carefully she gathered them up and replaced them in the Hessian bag, tightened the drawstring, laid the bag under her pillow and slept until the sun rose.

# Unholy Joy

"Unholy Joy" was one of five stories with the umbrella title *Food For Thought*. It was produced by the BBC in Bristol by Viv Beeby and was transmitted in 2000. The reader was Bill Wallis.

It was not until some time afterwards that Jake fully understood how much he had hated his master. He had been conceived and born into the hatred. He had witnessed it in the faces of his mother and his father and of the other servants.

The master, being a second son, had received only a small inheritance, part of which was the lease of the house in which he lived and where he tried to match the lifestyle of his wealthier neighbours.

One of the ways in which he stretched his pennies and his pounds was by requiring each member of his staff to serve in more than one capacity. The nursemaid must also be governess. The groom, valet. The kitchen skivvy doubled as chambermaid and the cook, who in addition to her culinary duties acted as housekeeper, and found work for any briefly idle hands. As a consequence the best and most able servants stayed at the house for only as long as it took them to find positions in more promising establishments. Those who remained were sad creatures. Jake's mother had been lame. His father coughed. The chambermaid skivvy had a walleye and the housekeeper's ruddy checks suggested a regular misappropriation of the cooking sherry.

As a boy Jake had spent little time at school for he had been required to serve as beater in the shooting season, stable lad and valet when the gentlemen rode to hounds and farm labourer at harvest times. When Jake's father had lain down in his bed above the tackle room and quietly died, Jake, at fifteen, had been expected to assume his duties.

The master, irritated by the loss of an experienced older man, had been intolerant of the boy's efforts and chastised him, lashing him with his tongue and sometimes with his riding crop.

At about this time the master married. He fathered six children in as many years and there would have been more had not his young wife's health failed.

The babies became children and the mistress watched as Jake lifted them into their saddles, taught them how to hold their reins and manage their ponies, comforted them when they took a fall and encouraged them when they were required to demonstrate their horsemanship to their critical father.

By the time Jake's mother joined his father under a wooden cross in the churchyard, Jake was in charge of the stable and the gunroom. It was he who, before the hunt set off for a day of killing, distributed the stirrup cups. The master, his huge horse plunging, would snatch his drink, toss it down his wide throat and hurl the empty cup in Jake's direction, daring him to fumble the catch.

Because his master's eyes were cruel, Jake avoided them. Once, as a small boy, he had looked full into the man's face and had felt his spirits shrivel, his blood curdle. He had lowered his head and looked away as the other servants looked away, as his mother and his father had looked away whenever the master turned in their direction.

Years passed. The children rode to hounds, found partners at the hunt balls. Married. Except for Rupert, the eldest, a quiet boy who resembled his mother.

The master grew stout, his face flushed and his neck purpled. He cursed as Jake struggled to hoist him up into his saddle. As the master became heavy his wife appeared more fragile beside him. When the other ladies gathered on the portico to watch the departure of the hunt, Jake would glimpse her at an upstairs window, her face a pale blur, her eyes on her husband's broad back as he rode away.

And if it had been true, when she claimed that the weal on her cheek was caused by a briar, flicking back during her regular walk through the shrubbery, or that the mark on her arm had been made when a door had been caught and slammed by the wind. And if her pier-glass really had swung forward, striking and bruising her temple, then the raised voices the servants sometimes heard must have been no more than the master's lively conversations with her when he and she were alone in the privacy of her chamber. But Jake knew otherwise and began to experience a curious sensation. A protectiveness, a feeling, though he hardly dared acknowledge it, of intolerable anger, was building, unrecognised, inside him.

He continued about his business, the days so full that he had little energy for contemplation of the situation. The new stable boy was sickly, so Jake must oversee the spreading of the fresh straw, the grooming of the hunters, the polishing of the tackle, the cleaning of the guns. When the master and his cronies returned from their days of sport, muddying the floors as they clattered into the house to fall, blowing and wheezing, into the chairs around the fire, Jake must be there with the mulled wine, Jake must haul off the muddy boots, collect the soiled coats, run the baths. Jake must wait at the supper table, dispense the port, and as often as not help his reeling employer to his bed and tend his hangover next morning, while the man vented his ill-temper by reducing to tears the timid new chambermaid, Isabelle.

One October day the master was carried home from the

hunting field insensible on a gate, four of the farm boys staggering under the weight of him. Unseated by a dizzy spell, he had fallen and stunned himself. Doctor Parker was called. The injuries were of little consequence but a mild condition of the heart was diagnosed and some pills were prescribed, which the patient must place beneath his tongue in the event of subsequent attacks.

Restored, the master took his place as usual at the head of his table for the hunt supper, where, after the ladies had withdrawn, the gentlemen would roar the night away.

Jake noticed, as he served the mistress with her soup, a fresh discoloration on her wrist. Aware of the direction of his eyes, she moved her arm so that the lace of her sleeve concealed the bruise. His hand shook and the soup ladle clattered in the tureen. The blade of the carving knife was bright in the lamplight as he placed its bone handle into his master's palm and stood back watching as the huge man drove it through the roasted meat.

On several occasions over the succeeding weeks, Jake was to see his master's face blanch, beads of sweat forming as he groped in his waistcoat pocket for his medication. Responding quickly, he would soon regain his breath, the colour flooding back into his face as the tiny pill took effect.

The discomfort he suffered did nothing to improve his temper. He bawled at the cook, slapped the skivvy, cuffed the stable lad and scowled at Jake.

On a raw November afternoon the shooting party returned early. The mistress, concerned for her husband's health, followed him into his dressing room and, when Jake entered it, on his way to draw his master's bath, several warmed towels over his arm, she came past him through the doorway. She did not speak and moved quickly away, but not before her servant had seen the reddened imprint of an open palm across her cheek. Jake felt the familiar anger surge through him as he filled the bathtub. Failing to get a response to his knock on the master's door, he opened it. The large man was sprawled half-naked in a chair. His mouth gaped soundlessly and his and eyes rolled in his livid face. Arms and legs flailed as he groped without success for the pill box in the pocket of his waistcoat, which lay where he had thrown it, on the floor.

In seconds Jake had placed the pill under his master's tongue and was watching it take effect. Soon, his discomfort turning to anger, the master had recovered enough for Jake to help him to his bed, settle him against his pillows and, as instructed, leave him, the pill box safely in his palm, a tumbler of water close at hand.

That night Jake had no appetite for food. The other servants, mopping gravy from their plates with thick slices of dry bread, stared, concerned for him.

As Jake had watched the master recover from this most recent and severe attack, it had come to him, with a sensation that took his own breath away, that he might so easily have withheld the drug, let the sick man choke and gasp his way to hell, or at the very least to purgatory. But like a mindless puppet he had obeyed his master. He could have rid them, all of them, from mistress to skivvy, of the tyrant in whose shadow they crept and scurried through their lives. Instead he had allowed the habit of his own lifetime to prolong his master's. He had failed the mistress. Failed the stable boy. Failed the innocent, bewildered Isabelle, who was already beginning to wilt under the master's bleak stare and vicious tongue. Next time. Next time he would do it. But who knew how long it would be before another such opportunity presented itself? But he would do it. He would. The certainty made him tremble and sweat.

A bell-pull was tugged somewhere in the house, and the silence was broken in the kitchen as the spring bounced and the bronze tongue clattered. Isabelle rose at once to answer the summons. Muffins for Master Rupert, perhaps. Moments later she returned, white-faced.

"It's the master!" she whispered. "You'm to fetch the doctor, Jake!"

He was one of the eight men who carried the heavy coffin through the churchyard where the servants lined the path. He helped lower it into the grave around which the family was grouped.

Later, when the guests had gone, he lit the lamps in the crêped drawing room where the mistress sat with her children, their faces and their hands pale against the dark fabric of their mourning clothes. He kept his eyes lowered in case they read his thoughts.

In the kitchen the servants stood, still dressed for the funeral in their coats and hats. The cook was flushed. The walleyed skivvy trembled. The stable boy gnawed his knuckles. Isabelle had removed her bonnet and stood, her smooth hair shining in the lamplight as Jake came into the room and looked from one to the other of them.

It was the stable boy who broke the silence.

"Master's dead!" he breathed, scared to say the words aloud.

"Dead, Jake!" the walleyed woman echoed.

"Gone forever!" gurgled the cook.

Then they stood, transfixed, the clock ticking, until all of a sudden the stable boy hauled off his cap, sent it spinning high into the air and let out a great whoop of glee. The skivvy, her one good orb lit with an unholy joy, squealed, and hugging herself began to caper stiffly round and round the kitchen. The cook threw back her head, cackled with laughter and collapsed heavily onto a chair.

"For gawd's sake let me sit," she wheezed. "Afore I piss meself!"

In the drawing room the family heard the distant eruption of sound and turned to one another, considering what it could be, while in the kitchen Jake had raised a forefinger to his lips and been instantly obeyed. The family settled against their cushions and the silence fell back into place around them as gently as the silk of the women's dark skirts.

"We will respect the dead," Jake said soberly. "We have our work to attend to." Behind him the kitchen door was opened. As the servants stared, Jake turned and saw that Rupert, tall in his mourning suit, was standing in the doorway. He cleared his throat. The servants waited. The women smoothed their clothes, the stable boy stared.

"My father was unprepared for his death," the young man said, as though he had rehearsed his words. "And had made no provision in his will for you. But I believe he would have wished to reward you for your service to him." Then he gave each of then a guinea. Even the stable lad. Even Isabelle, who had been only a month in the house. The cook curtseyed and broke out in a sweat. The girls blushed. The stable boy gaped. Jake bowed.

"I am to be your master now," Rupert said, and Jake spoke up for all the servants, assuring the young man of their loyalty. The women bobbed, and the boy, following Jake's example, inclined his head respectfully. After their new master left them, closing the door quietly behind him, the silence in the kitchen was profound. Only the mistress had ever spoken so gently to them before, and none of the family had ever visited the kitchens. Bewildered, they looked to Jake for guidance through this unfamiliar state of affairs.

"The family will take a light supper in an hour," he said to the cook. "Fires must be lit in the bedrooms, Isabelle. And 'tis time the horses was fed, boy. You all knows your duties. Set about them if you please."

They scattered obediently, the stable lad polishing his coin against his sleeve, the women twittering with excitement.

As the old house creaked its way into the darkness it seemed, that night, to enfold its occupants more protectively than usual. In the kitchen, where the lamplight was soft on the faces of the servants, Jake found his gaze straying to Isabelle's ankles, her pink cheeks and clear blue eyes.

# Wreckage

"Wreckage" was commissioned as part of a group of stories with the umbrella title *Schooldays*. It was recorded in London by the BBC and transmitted in 2001. Sara Davies was the producer. The story was read by Susannah Harker.

At the base of the cliff, its steel skin stripped silver as fish scales, wreckage was lifted on each wave and flung, howling, into the mauling jaws of rocks. And then he had written—Ulrich—the German boy, had written—"Ich halte das nicht länger aus."

At kindergarten the children wore smocks that buttoned down their backs. On Fridays Jane took hers, crusted with poster paint and various glues, home to her mother who laundered it, ready for Monday. The children had milk and biscuits at eleven and took it in turn to tidy up afterwards, using the brush-and-crumb tray.

Two women owned the school. Miss Maurice, small, pink, plump, her hair a pale frizz, who in summer wore flimsy, floral frocks under which her soft flesh moved. Miss Cohen often dressed in trousers. She was tall and lean with close-cropped, iron-grey hair. If there were whispers about these women, Jane and the other children did not hear them.

Then the war began and Jane's home filled with her cousins, sent from London to avoid the blitz. Michael, the only boy, cut the letters H-I-T-L-E-R into the ebony sheen of the Bechstein piano, because Germans were bad. "The Allies" must defeat them. Only then could normal life be resumed and families reunited. There would be rubber balls again and bananas and crêpe-soled sandals. Every misfortune was a result of "the hostilities" and it was Hitler's fault when trains ran late or there was a dead mouse in the loaf.

One morning, after prayers, the headmistresses, side by side on the dais, described to their pupils what was happening to children in Nazi Germany. How they too were deprived of treats because of the war. And how Jewish children were being separated from their parents. The English children listened.

"There are many Jewish children," Miss Cohen said, "whose parents want them to be safe from the Gestapo. They would like us to take care of them in England until the war is over." She paused, measuring the effect of her words on her charges. Some of the older pupils exchanged glances, grappling with the concept. Children in trouble. But German children?

There were to be three of them. Miss Maurice, soft hips mobile under daisy dress, showed photographs. Ten-year-old Jutta's parents were in Amsterdam where her father was running an undercover clinic for refugees and Allied airmen shot down by the Luftwaffe. Hannah, the youngest of the three, was at present unsafely concealed in her grandmother's loft. These girls were to board at the school while for the third child, a boy named Ulrich, the headmistresses had obtained a place at a neighbouring boarding school for boys.

That day each child carried home a letter from Miss Maurice and Miss Cohen, setting out their proposal. Two pupils were removed from the school, perhaps because the prospect of German children among their own made the parents uneasy. Or because it was felt that the two head-mistresses, always unconventional, had, on this occasion, over-stepped the limits of acceptable behaviour. But the major-ity of parents proved both compliant and compassionate, perceiving the newcomers not as aliens but as fellow-vic-tims of the war.

The children arrived. Jutta was absorbed into a higher class than Jane's, while Hannah, only seven years old, mute and tearful, her brilliant, dark eyes stricken, took her place at the desk next to Jane's.

Hannah's hair was braided into thick, brown pigtails, each fastened with an elastic band. Jane, whose thin hair was blonde and straight, envied the dark tendrils that escaped from Hannah's plaits and formed fragile, lacy curls across her forehead and at the nape of her neck. Mothers came forward with their daughters' outgrown skirts and jerseys. Hannah began to respond to the warmth with which she was welcomed. Her classmates made a game of teaching her their language, holding up objects and repeating the nouns until she could reproduce them. "Book," "milk," "pencil" establishing a communication that developed with astonishing speed. Ribbons were found for Hannah's plaits and she began to smile, from the start settling more easily into her new surroundings than did Jutta or Ulrich, who, being older, were less innocent of the facts of the war.

Jane's mother invited the three of them to tea. Jutta was politely silent, disapproving of Hannah's easy response to her hosts. Ulrich, through the thick lenses of his steel-rimmed spectacles, explored the details of the house, focussing suddenly on the inscription on the piano.

"Michael did it!" Elizabeth said, still awed by her brother's fall from grace.

Ulrich's lenses flashed as he turned to the small, embarrassed boy. "But why did you this?" he demanded in his strange, new English. "You admire the Führer?" The word was disconcerting in this very English sitting room. Michael blushed and shook his head. Bombs were falling each night on London. His home and his parents were, he knew, in danger. He was confused. "Then why write his name where you must each day see it?" Ulrich persisted and Michael, who had been told he must befriend Ulrich and understood why, took his rosy lower lip between his teeth and said nothing.

"Ich halte das nicht langer aus."

That summer Hannah was everyone's darling. She joined Jane and her cousins for picnics on their beach. She went with them onto their gorse-covered headland and played hide-and-seek. When it rained they read their favourite stories to her, taught her their songs and learned hers.

After the war, unable to find any trace of her family, Miss Cohen and Miss Maurice adopted Hannah. Jutta, reunited with her parents, emigrated with them to Canada. But Ulrich...Ulrich.

The school where he boarded, and which Michael attended as a dayboy, had strong naval connections. The fathers, older brothers and uncles of many of its pupils were serving on minesweepers and destroyers protecting the North Atlantic convoys from German attack as they entered the Western Approaches. Whenever a famous British ship was lost the school marked the occasion with special prayers and a half-masted flag. As losses were mourned so victories were celebrated. When the *Graf Spee*, cornered by *Exeter*, *Ajax* and *Achilles*, was scuttled off Montevideo, Ulrich, with lowered eyes, mouthed the words of "He Who Would Valiant Be" as the jubilant school raised the chapel roof. After the German battleship *Admiral Scheer* sent the *Jervis Bay* to the bottom, he stood, head bowed, as his peers soberly sang "For Those In Peril On The Sea". But in the May of 1941, Ulrich had barely weathered the defection of Rudolph Hess, when HMS *Hood* and most of her crew was lost. This proved too much for his classmates. They closed their ears to his unforgivable accent and found it impossible to meet his expressionless eyes.

Days later news broke that British ships had driven the *Bismarck*, icon of the German fleet, into open water and pounded her with their guns until, mutilated, she slid under the debris-strewn surface of the oily sea.

Ulrich's narrow face closed while his fellows noisily discharged their patriotism and their pride. What his thoughts were no one knew or cared, assuming perhaps that as his kind were also suffering at the hands of the Nazis, his loyalty would lie with his British hosts.

The euphoria over the sinking of the *Bismarck* extended through several days of sultry weather, which broke down eventually into a violent summer storm. South-westerly gales and a spring tide made the beach dangerous and drove spray and spume high over the cliff tops. As the seas abated, wreckage was discovered, grinding and buckling in the shallows below the headland. Markings identified the debris as the remains of a German U-boat that had been destroyed, mid-Channel, some days previously.

Jane and her cousins were brought, together with other local children, rubber-booted and mackintoshed, to stare, some nervously, at this slain dragon and to revel in its humiliation, giving no thought to the men who had served and possibly perished in her. They were Germans. Enemies.

Ulrich stood, the drizzle misting his spectacles, while his classmates whooped and rejoiced, pointing and peering down at the wreckage where it writhed and twisted in the surf.

Then, as low cloud and a rising tide diminished the scene, the children were called away to trudge home to their tea.

Ulrich was found next day at the foot of the cliff. He did not appear to have fallen but somehow to have climbed down to the wreckage. Nor had he drowned, though his clothes were sodden after overnight rain.

If the cause of his death was ever established, Jane and her cousins were not told of it. A silence closed over the unfortunate incident. The attention of the children was drawn away, gently but firmly diverted from the subject of the boy, the German boy, who was dead.

Their lives began to fill with new preoccupations. First the bombings and then the war itself were over. The house emptied. The children separated and grew up.

Jane discovered the schoolbooks—hers, Michael's and Elizabeth's—in a box amongst a clutter of other childhood possessions. Then, on the cover of one and printed in an unfamiliar, Gothic hand, she read the name Ulrich Neimann. Inside were pages of neat exercises. At the foot of each, in red ink, were marks out of ten and comments in a teacher's rounded hand. On the last page, which was dated June the third, 1941, was a single sentence. The words were in German and Jane was unable to interpret them.

Later, at his sister's wedding, Jane, in her bridesmaid dress, asked Michael to translate.

"Ich halte das nicht langer aus," she repeated, carefully. Michael grimaced at her accent and watched as a waiter refilled his glass with champagne.

"Roughly," he said, "it means 'I cannot bear any more'. Why d'you ask?"

"Ulrich wrote it," Jane said, the name bridging the years. The wedding celebrations seemed to crystallise around them until she and Michael were standing, isolated, transported back to the headland and the rain and the wreck. "He wrote it a week after the *Bismarck* was sunk. The day before they found him dead."

They could see him there, standing on the cliff-top, looking down. His pale, narrow face, sleek hair and the steel-rimmed spectacles beaded by rain. Below him the noisy sea plundered the wreckage.

# Old Devil Moon

"Old Devil Moon" was recorded by the BBC in Bristol, transmitted in April 1997 and featured in *Pick Of The Week*. It was produced by Viv Beeby and the reader was Anthony Bate.

A decade of widowerhood had accustomed me to solitude. After my daughter Kay left home I had begun, guiltily at first, to relish my quiet house and self-indulgent ways. Well-meaning friends who had attempted, in the early days, to pair me with some kindred spirit, deprived by death or divorce of her spouse, now only rarely called upon me to make up numbers when they entertained.

Then I fell in love.

It happened that my cousin Ruth, short of a man at her dinner-party and bribing me with the promise of *bœuf en croûte*, had persuaded me from home. The other guests were paired except for one. She stood with her back to me, talking to a couple I did not know, heavy hair swinging to her shoulders. As she turned to face me and my cousin said, "Jack dear, meet Phoebe," my life was, quite simply, changed.

Needless to say I concealed the intensity of my reaction and during dinner paid her no more attention than the situation demanded. Phoebe had, my cousin later informed me, sotto voce, as she poured coffee, recently ended a relationship. She needed to get out and meet people without being pestered by pushy males.

I was careful not to push, confining myself to amusing Phoebe. Encouraging her to laugh, talk, feel at ease. And she responded. Without in any way neglecting our fellow-guests she made me feel…well…you may imagine how I felt. This glorious girl sitting beside me, paying attention to me, then seeking me out, brandy glass in hand, as we mingled after the meal, allowing me to entertain her. I was enchanted.

"Well," said Ruth, handing me my coat when the evening was over, her eyes challenging, mine evasive, "you certainly hit it off with Phoebe! Such a pity she's not…well…" Ruth decided to be blunt: "In the right age group."

It was true. Phoebe was half my age. Only a few years older than my daughter Kay, whom she knew socially and remembered as a junior in high school.

The silent emptiness of my house seemed less attractive after that dinner party, and when, two weeks later, my daughter and her husband invited me to join them and their friends for a lunchtime barbecue, I accepted gladly.

The summer weather was oppressive and thunderheads were massing over the downs. Kay and John's garden runs down to a river. The prospect of a swim was appealing, so, with a couple of bottles of well-chilled Chardonnay and my swimming things on the back seat of the car, I drove over.

I wasn't expecting Phoebe to be there, having forgotten that she and my daughter were acquainted. I had assumed we never would, never should, meet again. But there she was, perched like a naiad on the wooden jetty, draped in white towelling, her wet hair dripping down her back.

At six o'clock, as the party broke up, the heavens opened. Borrowing an umbrella from Kay, I ran, with Phoebe on my arm, through the downpour, to her car. The MG, an early 1960s' model, was, on Phoebe's own admission, highly unsuitable for someone without mechanical skills, but she adored it, called it Hermione and suffered a succession of breakdowns with equanimity.

"D'you like Italian?" she enquired, cranking down the

126

rain-spattered window and without waiting for my reply continued: "There's a great place in Chislethorpe." I nodded dumbly, smiling, I imagine, like a loon. "See you there," she said, depressing Hermione's accelerator, gravel flying from her spinning tyres.

The place was crowded. I found Phoebe at the bar sipping a dry Martini. Five minutes later we were shown to a corner table.

After that she and I met once, sometimes twice a week. A mutual passion for foreign films drew us from one corner of the county to the other. Side by side in the darkness, we patronised cinemas ranging from village fleapits to smart multiplexes. Fellini, Bergman, Adlon, Bertolucci. We watched and watched again.

On our first "date" Phoebe had insisted on paying for our supper, since she had, she reminded me, invited me to join her. I indulged her, taking my revenge a few weeks later by giving her dinner at Lovage's, a restaurant second only to the prohibitively expensive and internationally renowned Peacocks, which, in my fantasies, I was already reserving for a future and most particular occasion. She accepted the meal gracefully enough but always insisted on paying for her ticket when we went together to the cinema.

For months we enjoyed each other's company. I told her of my long and happy marriage and of my difficulty in making sense of life when Alice died. She discussed with me the three major love affairs that had convinced her that a successful long-term relationship would elude her. When I suggested that she might be happier with an older man, she laughed. We both laughed.

It seemed I had no choice but to live from day to day, reminding myself firmly that for Phoebe and me there could be nothing beyond our easy, Platonic friendship. Occasionally my willpower would falter and I would briefly indulge myself, imagining Phoebe in other circumstances. Fantasies in which the difference in our ages became irrelevant and we would move from friendship towards other joys.

So we continued, through the winter and on towards spring. We walked through snow on the downs, and along the windy, pebbled beaches of the south coast, lunching at country pubs. Once, after a sobering incident when Hermione, having slithered into a ditch one frosty night, had to be hauled out by my BMW, Phoebe, slightly shaken and very grateful, had kissed me, her lips soft and light on my cheek, the air around her flavoured, deliciously, by her scent. On another occasion, under mistletoe and cousin Ruth's sharp eyes, Phoebe hugged me and I briefly felt her narrow body in my arms, her smooth, cool cheek against mine.

In April, a month before my sixtieth birthday and over a fragrant plate of *moules marinières*, Phoebe casually enquired how I intended to celebrate the occasion. She was shocked when I protested that beyond one's fiftieth, birthdays are unworthy of celebration, for no sane person wishes to be reminded of the relentless march of time, the imminent grip of old age, the approach of death.

She chastised me, her emphasis startling diners at neighbouring tables. "What rubbish, Jack! You're in your prime! It's so unfair! Women lose the precious bloom of youth while you men simply acquire an interesting patina!"

The subject was dropped. Phoebe put her cheek against mine when, one evening, we were searching the skies for a particular star... . A few days later, after watching *Jules et Jim*, she linked her arm through mine and solemnly invited me to dine with her on my birthday. I accepted of course. She refused to tell me where we were to eat but there was a suppressed excitement about her that convinced me it was to be Peacocks. Peacocks! Famous for its eccentric host, its world-beating specialities, and above all for its ambience. The Gothic building was reputed to overlook floodlit gardens where fountains plashed into an ornamental lake. Where the scent of roses…honeysuckle…lilies, drifted through the galleried dining rooms. This was where the rich came to impress. Where famous lovers exchanged their vows.

I ordered a new suit. It was cut from a fine, charcoal-grey wool, had soft shoulders and a fashionable fluidity of line. I had to admit, as I scrutinised my appearance in the tailor's long looking glass, that it flattered me. A barber in Jermyn Street persuaded me to wear my hair slightly longer at the nape of my neck than was my habit.

Phoebe's plan was to pick me up in Hermione and drive me to our secret destination.

The evening was still, after an unusually warm spring day. I was ready an hour too soon and so nervous that I took a stiff Scotch as I listened for the sound of Hermione's erratic engine.

I'm unsure what my hopes were for that evening but I had blanked out my doubts and was certain that by the end of it my relationship with Phoebe would have progressed from merely friendship, however delightful that had been, to something else. Something I hardly dared imagine. Phoebe had revived me. Kick-starting emotions that had been buried first by grief and then by time. I was no longer an ageing widower, sidelined into a quiet decline. Boosted by the whisky, my self-confidence burgeoned. What did age matter! For almost a year Phoebe and I had been virtually inseparable…linked by shared interests and, obviously, by a mutual attraction. Had she not taken my arm, straightened my tie? Kissed me even? And she had planned, for my birthday, a magical evening. I would, of course, pretend to be surprised when we swept in, through the wrought-iron gates to Peacocks! The Scotch burned reassuringly down. I spread my fingers. Not a tremor. Steady as a rock. Calm. Masterful. And rose to my feet as the sound of the car reached me.

In the drive Phoebe leaned across to open the passenger door. Her lips wished me a happy birthday and touched mine. Then I was buckling my seatbelt as the car plunged forward, lurched down the drive and squealed out, onto the main road.

She drove fast, with her usual exhilarating flair, in the direction of the restaurant. The hood was down. A warm slipstream, smelling of primroses and May blossom, poured past us. Conversation was impossible so from time to time we smiled at one another through the roaring air.

"Small detour," Phoebe yelled, wrenching the wheel. "Left my jacket at Kay's. Need it for tomorrow. Won't take a second. Okay?"

Of course it was okay. Nothing that Phoebe could ever do would not be okay. "She loves me," I thought. "She knows what I'm feeling, what I'm planning. I won't push her. I won't pin her down or be possessive. But our relationship will change. Has to change. She wants it to change. And tonight, at Peacocks, we will decide how it will change."

She took the car swiftly up the familiar lane to Kay's house, where a solitary light in an upstairs room glimmered through the twilight.

When there was no response to Phoebe's knock on the

front door she turned her concerned face to me. I suggested that Kay and John might be down by the river. We skirted the house, the profound silence broken only by the sound of our footsteps, crushing the gravel. The jetty was deserted.

Behind the house the terrace lay in shadow. There seemed to be something white on the long, garden table. I stared at it, trying to discern what it was, Phoebe at my elbow. The table, I realised, was laden with a feast. There were platters of food, piles of plates, groups of glasses and clusters of napkins folded prettily into water-lily shapes.... Suddenly the scene erupted violently with sound and light. People poured out, bellowing and laughing, through the open doors of the house.

I stood, transfixed. Phoebe, facing me now, was smiling. Laughing at my gobsmacked expression.

"Surprise!" she shouted. It was the word the others were howling all around me. Kay, John, cousin Ruth, acquaintances, neighbours…streaming out of the house, drinks in their hands, grinning, laughing, leering, pumping my hand, slapping my back… "Surprise!" they roared. "Surprise!" Phoebe put her arms round me and kissed me on both cheeks.

"Happy sixtieth, dear old Jack! Happy sixtieth…"

I managed, of course, to put a good face on it. There were hours of eating, drinking, dancing even. At the end of it Phoebe was judged to be unfit to drive and it was decided that she should stay overnight with Kay and that cousin Ruth would take me home.

For miles I watched the familiar road unwinding in the relentless glare of the headlights.

"Such a darling girl," Ruth said at last, with a brief, sharp glance in my direction. Trying, I knew, to read me, then sulkily resigning herself to my silence. "And so fond of you, Jack! Tonight was her idea, you know!"

I can still see their faces. I shall always see their faces. Blurred, except for Phoebe's face. I can still hear their voices and through them, Phoebe's voice.

"Happy sixtieth. Dear-Old-Jack."

# The Swimming Lesson

"The Swimming Lesson" was one of a group of *Scottish Shorts* recorded by BBC Scotland Radio Drama and transmitted in January 2003. The reader was Joanna Tope and the programme was produced in Glasgow by Bruce Young.

On the first of August each year the family arrived, driving out from their rich house in the suburbs of Glasgow for their holiday at the crofter's cottage. At first they had come in horse-drawn carriages, now in shiny, head-turning motorcars, the boys wearing sailor suits, a nursemaid, cook and parlour maid in summer uniforms, the mother and Isobel, the youngest child, with muslins for the warmest days, their father sporting tweeds and linen.

While the parents walked on the headland or lazed in the shade of pine trees that grew around the sheltered cove, the five sons and one daughter fished from rocks or rowing boat and waded through the cold, clear water, probing rock pools for crabs. Some days they straddled plump ponies and rode up onto the heathery hills. Before breakfast each morning, and regardless of the weather, those who were able accompanied their father on a compulsory swim across the cove.

At the end of the first week the family and its retainers gathered at dusk for a ceremony of initiation, for on the holiday of their seventh year, each child was required to climb into the boat, which their father would row out into the centre of the cove and then, on his order, to leap obediently from its transom. One after another, year after year, they had risen gasping to the surface of the cold water, arms flailing, and had struck out, back towards the shore. Isobel had heard her father's laugh as he swivelled the little boat and followed first Angus, then David, then James, then Rupert, then Marcus, as they spluttered desperately towards the watchers on the shingle, where their mother, regardless of wet shoes and damp hem, would pluck them, shuddering, from the shallows, envelop them in a rug woven in the family tartan, and drawing them close to the driftwood fire rub her hands over their ribs to warm them.

"But he cannot swim!" she had protested on each successive occasion.

"Then he will learn!" their father shouted. And learn they did, dog-paddling fast through the chill, still water, reaching down at last with numbed feet for the slippery pebbles.

Isobel was unsure when she had first become aware of the ritual, and could barely remember the occasion of Angus's initiation, as she had been little more than an infant at that time—but as the years had turned and each of her brothers reached his seventh, the ceremony had become more vivid, more terrifying, for inevitably, one day, the small figure crouching in the boat, awaiting their father's command, would be hers.

Between her sixth birthday and the date of the family's holiday Isobel's anxiety grew. She dreamed of seaweed and woke, screaming. She ran a low fever. The family physician made her cough and say "ah". He assured her parents that a visit to the seaside would soon restore their daughter to her usual, robust health.

August arrived. Their prosperous father, enriched by business ventures on the Clyde, drove his family in the latest Hispano-Suiza up over the highlands and down the mountain to the bay. But for Isobel the enchantment of the place was, that year, tarnished by dread of her approaching ordeal.

Angus, watching her react to the sight of the swimming cove, considered ways in which he might help her. He knew their father would not relent, nor would their mother dare oppose him. The first day passed. The second and the third. Isobel could not eat. She barely slept.

On the fourth night the moon was full. The mountains casting black shadows and the surface of the swimming cove shining smooth as a looking glass.

When the house was quiet Angus came to Isobel's room. Silently, while the nursemaid snored, he took his sister's hand, drew her from her bed and out across the wet grass to the shore.

Because their feet were already chilled, the sea felt almost warm. But as the level rose past shin and thigh the cold snatched at their breath.

Isobel had paddled and even waded but she had never swum. Their father's way regarding swimming lessons had prevailed. Not only did his will dictate that sudden, total immersion in freezing water was the only way to acquire both the ability to swim and a courageous temperament, but the ceremony amused him.

When the water reached Isobel's chest Angus put his palm under her chin while she dog-paddled. He made her fill her lungs with air until she felt her own buoyancy and found her balance in the water. When at last he withdrew his hand and she moved forward, horizontal and unsupported, following him as he backed away from her, the shivering conspirators smiled.

On the day of the swim Angus spoke quietly to her. "Breathe in. Fill your lungs. Take your nose between finger and thumb. Jump with your feet together and your knees bent. As soon as you surface, strike out for the shore. Look at mother. Keep your eyes on her. You can do it, Issie! You can!"

The day had been warm, the smooth sea was iridescent with the colours of the sunset. Their mother said that Isobel should not be made to swim. It was too soon after her illness. She was a girl. She should be excused...

The boat lurched as their father settled his weight on the centre thwart and grasped the oars. Isobel climbed shakily aboard and sat in the stern, while her father, facing her, squinted into the low sunlight. She stared at the floorboards where the fishing lines were tangled and a crab, caught for bait, lay dismembered.

The rowlocks creaked and with each vigorous pull on the oars the boat surged forward. Above the lisp of water along the hull Isobel could hear the breath whistling through their father's hirsute nostrils. She felt sick. She prayed for death. Now. In the comparative comfort of the boat. Not in the dark water, which was slipping away, under the keel.

She felt the boat slow. They had reached the centre of the cove. Water was dripping from the rested oars. At any moment she would hear their father's voice.

"Right, young lady. Let's see what you are made of!" But he did not speak. The dismembered crab rolled in the rocking boat. Isobel's heart was thumping out the seconds. Surely their father could hear it? She gripped the gunwale. Soon she must stand and force first one foot and then the other up onto the aft thwart. There was a strange hissing inside her head. She closed her eyes. Perhaps God was answering her prayer and she was dying. Then she heard another sound, a curious, choking gasp. Her eyes flew open, found her father's face and widened at what she saw.

In the strange colours of the sunset his skin was livid, his eyes rolled and he gulped air like a dying fish. The oars were clattering from his grasp. He was clutching his throat and struggling to his feet. The little boat lurched wildly as he lost his balance and pitched into the sea.

Isobel clambered towards their father, leaned out and reached for him. He caught her by the wrist, pulling her down towards him, his mottling face close to hers, seawater pouring over the gunwale. His fingers were like steel, crushing her bones. She shut her eyes and clenched her teeth on the pain. Then she felt his grip loosen and slip. She caught at his slackening hand, and gripping it in both of hers braced herself and held him until Angus and the ghillie reached the boat.

Their father was carried into the house and laid on a table. Seawater beaded tendrils of his hair and beard and ran from his sodden clothes. The ghillie closed his eyes and the housekeeper placed candles around the rim of the table. Their mother and the older boys sat with him until the candles had burned down and the long night gave way to a grey dawn.

They were to be fetched home. Their father was to be funeralled and put into the ground.

Isobel stared across the swimming cove. The little boat lay above the tide line. Angus joined her, his footsteps crunching the shingle.

"I want to do it," she said. "I want to swim."

They slid the boat into the shallows, Isobel pulled on her bathing dress and climbed aboard.

The rising sun cleared the mountain as she stood on the transom, steadied herself, took her nose between finger and thumb, filled her lungs and jumped clean and straight, plunging down, the cold burning into her. She opened her eyes, and looking upwards as she rose through the water saw the fractured underside of its surface, and beyond it blue sky and white cloud. She broke into the air, dog-paddling and kicking hard towards the shore. Her eyes were stinging but she could see their mother, the plaid rug in her hands.

Isobel stood, wrapped and rubbed, teeth chattering, the taste of the sea sharp in her mouth, and was conscious only of the image of her father, cold and still on the table.

"Good child," their mother murmured. "For your father's sake. I understand. Now go indoors and dress warmly." But as she watched her daughter go, the rug clutched tightly round her, the mother felt suddenly uncertain.

Isobel's nursemaid towelled her dry, eased fleecy bodice and woollen dress over her head, combed out her damp hair and braided it while the child sat, staring at her reflection, at the firm line of her jaw and at her steady, level, dry eyes, and knew that it was not for her father's sake that she had swum.

Angus came and stood behind her, his eyes meeting hers in the looking glass. Both were aware of the likeness between the powerful, dark man who had been their father and his youngest child, this small daughter.

"I didn't swim for him," Isobel said via the mirror.

Angus searched her face. "Then why did you?"

She said she did not know and for some time this was true. But as she grew and time levelled the memories of their father, she began to understand herself. Then she knew.

One evening, when she and Angus were visiting the cottage with their own, growing children, she told him.

They were in the rowing boat, their thoughts, like the mackerel lines in their hands, drifting back.

"It was not for Father, Angus. It was for me," she said. "I believed he would have thought I used his death as an excuse not to swim. I wasn't going to let him leave me with that guilt."

They sat, their reflected faces swimming in the dark water. There was something of her father in her, they knew it. Something of his spirit and his power. "A certain ruthlessness of soul," Angus had once called it. The silence spread away from them.

Their children had lit a fire on the shingle. Small voices occasionally reached them. Minute by minute, as the light faded, the flames grew brighter.

"It was barbaric, Issie," Angus said. "Barbaric. But you were wise to do it." He paused. "I would have stayed dry and regretted it later."

"It was easier for me."

"Why?"

"Perhaps because I had a better teacher than you did."

They smiled and shuddered, remembering the full moon and the swimming lesson in the dark, cold, water. Remembering the brutish father and the weak mother. Now, at this distance, they could accept them. Love them, even.

Angus turned the boat towards the shore.